The Hippie in the Wall

Also by Tony Fennelly:

The Glory Hole Murders

The Closet Hanging

The Hippie in the Wall

Tony Fennelly

St. Martin's Press
New York

THE HIPPIE IN THE WALL. Copyright © 1994 by Tony Fennelly. All rights reserved. Printed in the United States of America. No part of this book may be used or reproduced in any manner whatsoever without written permission except in the case of brief quotations embodied in critical articles or reviews. For information, address St. Martin's Press, 175 Fifth Avenue, New York, N.Y. 10010.

Design by Basha Zapatka

Library of Congress Cataloging-in-Publication Data

Fennelly, Tony.
    The hippie in the wall / Tony Fennelly.
      p. cm.
    ISBN 0-312-10475-8
    1. Women detectives—Louisiana—New Orleans—Fiction. 2. New Orleans (La.)—Fiction. I. Title.
PS3556.E49H57   1994
813'.54—dc20   93-44032
                                                            CIP

First Edition: June 1994
10 9 8 7 6 5 4 3 2 1

To the Clintons:

How about inviting me to the White House?!
    I write good mysteries.
    I voted for y'all.
    And I have a cat!

The Hippie in the Wall

Prologue

Bourbon Street;
February 13, 1991

"Poor bugger must have been sealed up in there twenty years."

Only two square feet of cedar paneling had been pried away, just enough to expose the head and torso of the skeleton. Curly blond hair still adhered to the whitish skull now grinning inside the splintered frame as though gazing through a window.

Lieutenant Frank Washington, of NOPD Homicide, held his linen handkerchief up to his face and spoke through it.

"Yeah, about that."

"Twenty?" Officer Curtis Prout stayed behind him. He was detailed to the French Quarter and had been the first cop called to the scene. "How do you figure?"

"He's wearing a flowered body shirt and striped bell-bottom jeans. Remember those?"

"Yeah, I had a pair myself. Mine were hip huggers so either sex could wear them."

"So are his. Or hers."

"Hey, Frank?" Prout pointed. "Look at what's hanging around his neck."

"I noticed—I can't even remember the last time I saw a peace symbol."

Washington stepped out to the cement courtyard behind the grandly misnamed Cabaret Paree. Three rough wooden doors, nearly denuded of their green paint, afforded the only egress at ground level. Rusted iron steps climbed up the brick wall to the sagging second-story balcony.

"This club has had at least a dozen names and owners since the hippie era. When I first came in here . . ." He sidestepped an empty beer keg. "It was Madame Julie's."

"That right, Frank? And just what was a righteous guy like you doing in a strip joint?"

"Back then . . ." He folded the handkerchief. "There was this girl called Cherry working here. She made an indelible impression on me."

"Yeah? And what was so special about this girl called Cherry?"

"My first naked white woman."

The nearest of the wooden doors opened on creaking hinges and a lanky transsexual stripper leaned out of her dressing room, wrapped in a terry cloth robe.

"Yoo-hoo, officers?" She wrinkled her long nose. "I always *thought* it smelled bad backstage."

"You were right."

One

It was still light out on Bourbon Street, and the old club was open for drinks only. The show (if a "show" you can call it) wouldn't start till eight. I stopped just inside the door to get accustomed to the dimness and wish I were anywhere else.

A tired crone who looked like a refugee from a bad Appalachian marriage was tending bar in front of the bare stage.

She awarded me a half-lidded glance. "You lookin' for a job?"

"Boy, it *must* be dark in here—I'm meeting Lieutenant Washington."

"Table in the back."

"Could I have a fountain Coke?"

Now I spotted Frank as a bulky shadow at the rearmost of the tables behind the iron railing. A long time ago I would lean across that same railing to take orders for zombies and hurricanes, tourist drinks.

I ran my hand along the row of empty barstools, negotiating the narrow aisle between bar and tables. The club was crammed with lilliputian furniture to allow seating for more paying customers than fire laws allowed, but they probably broke the capacity ordinance only on Mardi Gras.

My host popped up in greeting. "Margo Fortier!"

"Good evening, Frank."

I recalled the first time I'd seen Frank at that same table. He was a college football player back then, strong and lean, with a 'fro that must have popped out of his helmet whenever he took it off after a scrimmage.

He bent and pulled out a chair for me. "Thank you for coming."

Today he was too heavy for athletics and probably on medication for high blood pressure. The 'fro was gray and thinning, so he'd grown himself a mustache to compensate.

"No thanks are in order." I put my snakeskin purse down on his platter-size table and accepted the miniature chair but did *not* make myself comfortable. "I work for the paper and you told me there's a story here."

I didn't have to say, he probably guessed, that I'm frothing to break out of airhead society gossip and start reporting real news.

"Yes, there are a lot of stories here." Frank embraced the whole dingy arena with a sweep of his arm. "And one of them was yours. Remember all those nights you shook your little money maker up on that very stage?"

"That was twenty-one years ago."

"But it never changes. Have you noticed?"

The barmaid delivered our drinks, omitting the napkins but not the tip tray. Frank gave her four of his hard-earned dollars and she left us alone. He had settled for soda with lime. My Coke was good and strong.

"Nuts, I haven't been inside this place since . . ." I looked around at the red-flocked wallpaper. The club was darker and shabbier than the Madame Julie's I remembered. Or did it just seem that way? I'd always lived at night back then.

Frank persisted. "You were some wild dancer. You had the most revealing act on the street as I recall."

"On the contrary, I was relatively tame."

"But you stripped right down to the legal minimum. The other girls always kept their bra and panties on."

"That was another time, Frank."

"So?"

"So whenever those fine southern ladies saw a black face in the audience, they would get all of a sudden modest."

He stiffened with belated indignation. "Really?"

"We used to argue about it in the dressing room."

"Hell, I'd paid my lousy two fifty-five for the drink."

"Which was top price, by the way. The white customers usually got in for a buck fifty."

"Damn! I was entitled to see as much as anyone else."

"That was my position."

"You had other positions, too, and believe me, a poor Dillard student appreciated them." Frank looked over to the little stage as though a phantasm of a twenty-four-year-old me were still up there, frantically bumping and grinding to the beat of "Night Train."

I looked away from it, addressed my Coke, and drank through the straw so as not to put my hands on the cold, sweating glass.

"Say, Frank, what's the opposite of *nostalgia?*"

"How's that?"

"Some word that means a place you *don't* want to go back to. A past you would hope never to relive."

"I don't know the word, Cherry—Margo—but I know the feeling. All a man would retrieve from his youth is the virility. Everything else, the restlessness, the insecurity, is gladly put behind."

"And I've been Mrs. Julian Fortier for a lot of years now." I folded my arms in sleeves of pastel mink. "I've earned the name and the distance from Cherry and this whole cruddy scene."

"Sure, I understand, but bear with me a minute." Frank reached into his pocket and brought out a photograph.

"Here's the story I promised: In June 1970, the owner of this building, one Gerald Levin, got a permit to build an addition in the courtyard back there." He waved behind him.

"Yes, I remember Gerald needed more storage space."

"The plans included a vented cedar closet."

"For his wife's ball gowns. So what?"

"So the present owner of this building is a Mr. George Folkes, and last week *he* got a permit to tear that same addition down." He handed the photo over. "The demolition crew found this in the back wall of the closet." Then he gave me his penlight so I'd have a clear view of the exhibit: a full-color shot of a leering skull with blond hair.

"Cute." I clicked off the light.

"You might have met that man before he went into the wall."

"No, I'm sure I'd remember *him*."

"He would have been heavier." Frank left the photo on the table between us.

"So the poor unfortunate was part of the building for twenty-one years?" I reached into my purse for pad and pen. "You're right. It's a terrific story."

"Unfortunately, you have to be part of it." He held up a brown finger. "See, the ownership of this building has changed four times since the addition went up. Plus, this club has been leased to nine different managers over the years, and there are no written records of employees extant. But I remember"—now the finger leveled—"that *you* were here back when it was Madame Julie's . . . And something else."

"What?"

He grinned like a kid. "You're the *only* one I remember."

"I see the quid pro here. You want me to tell you who else was working in the club that spring."

"You're my only source."

"I'm flattered. But no thanks."

His brow wrinkled into gray lines. "Why? What's the problem?"

"You know bloody well what's the problem! I can't let it get around that Julian Fortier's wife made a living waving her bare ass at the drinking public. So it simply never happened."

I shot a finger of my own right back at him. "And as you just admitted, there are no records that prove I ever worked in this club." I slammed my pad on the table. "And I can sue your butt for libel if you say I did."

"Hold on there!" Frank held out his palm in a Stop sign. "I don't want to stir up a scandal. So you never set foot in here before, right? You're just a curious reporter nosing around for an exclusive."

"Huh?" I looked him up and down; he had put on his "innocent" face. "Then I'm not connected with this case at all."

"You?" He made a *pfff* sound. "Goodness, no."

"So anything I tell you won't have come from me."

"Certainly not. I got it telepathically through the air."

"Fair enough." I wrote "June of seventy" on my pad, then tapped the forensic photo. "But first, what do we know so far?"

"The victim was killed by two or three blows to the back of the head. The weapon could have been a tire iron or a crowbar. The killer propped him against the back wall, nailed his shirtsleeves to the studs to hold him up, added sand and lime, then installed the cedar panels over him."

"Then no one noticed that the finished closet measured short of the plan."

"Nearly a foot short. Apparently no one did."

"And wouldn't a decomposing corpse smell awful?"

"To high heaven. But the hidden compartment had a vent placed up near the ceiling, so most of the gasses would have been dispersed into the atmosphere."

That was more detail than I needed.

"What do you know about the man himself?"

"No ID on him." Frank produced a pad of his own, bigger than mine, and read from it. "But we know it was a white male, about twenty-two, close to six feet tall. The hair was light blond, so the eyes were probably blue. And from the size of his clothes, we conclude that he was well nourished. Forget fingerprints."

"You'll have to ID him through dental records."

"That's doubtful, as the teeth are perfect. Not so unusual for a man that young."

"DNA strip testing?"

"We can't get a conclusive readout from bones that old. Besides, there would be nothing to compare it to. We still have no idea who he's *supposed* to be."

"Labels in the clothes?"

"Gimbel's. A New York department store that's been out of business for some years."

"Then he wasn't even local. Just one of the millions of tourists and transients who blow through the Quarter every year. Good luck to you."

"I guess I was looking for a miracle, Margo." Frank finished his soda and removed the glass to the table behind us. "The impossibility that you would remember a hippie who stopped in for a drink twenty-one years ago and never left."

I clicked on his penlight for another look at the photo, covering the skull face with my finger.

"Half the boys on the street looked like . . . Hey, he wasn't *too* much of a hippie. He had short hair."

"Short?"

"For the time and culture. It barely hit his collar."

"That hadn't occurred to me. Maybe he was a recent convert. So you've just heard all I know. Now it's your turn." Frank uncapped his pen, which was a cheap one. "Tell me about the other dancers."

I closed my eyes and reviewed the lineup in my mind. Six girls were in the show that month.

"Five girls were in the show that month."

"Five?" He accepted the number neutrally. "Names?"

"We were all too shy to use our real ones. Stripping wasn't considered respectable back in 1970."

"I suspect there was more shyness about paying taxes than giving scandal, but go ahead."

"Kathy Hoffman was the headliner because she had these gorgeous C-cup bosoms. I checked her for scars, too. They were natural."

"Really? I hardly remember that kind. What else did she look like?"

"Blond, wholesome. She used to prance around in a blue cheerleader's outfit and twirl a baton."

"I recall the baton. She dropped it on me once." Frank rubbed his head with the recollection. "That girl looked like a real cheerleader, too."

"She *had* been a real one back in East Jesus, Ohio. Kathy left behind a Dick and Jane life and ran off to the city to look for excitement."

"Did she find it?"

"She did, in capsule form. Poor Kathy always carried a drugstore in her purse. Her motto was 'When in doubt, drop.'"

Frank was writing. "Where is she now?"

"Nowhere. The chick took a header off the Greater New Orleans Bridge back in '73."

Frank stopped writing. "That doesn't rule her out as a lead. But let's concentrate on the girls who are still alive."

"Fair enough. Do you remember Samantha? She used to wear a purple negligee decorated with paper stars and half-moons."

"Oh, yes. She did a 'Bewitched' number. Twitched her nose instead of . . ."

"Right. Her real name was Eileen Herd, but she called herself Samantha because she actually thought she *was* a witch."

"An odd delusion. Do you know what she's doing now?"

"A few months ago, I caught her telling fortunes in a New Age shop in Metairie."

"Still deluded then, but at least she'll be easy to find. Who else?"

"Sheila Casey always went on first. Do you recall an athletic redhead in orange spangles?"

Frank held his palms out in the Gallic gesture of nonrecollection.

"Sheila had been a high school gymnast and always finished her act with a split."

He scratched his head. "Sounds familiar somehow. Where and when have I seen that act?"

"Maybe two blocks down. Maybe last night. You see, Sheila is the only one of us who never left Bourbon Street."

"You're kidding."

"Catch her any night at Diamond Lil's." I watched as he made the notation in shorthand. "And something about it is really weird, Frank. As long as I've known that girl, she hasn't changed her hair or her moves. And every time she gets a new costume she has it made just like every one she had before. If you look at her under the soft lights of the club, you'd almost think she hadn't aged a day in twenty years."

"Why is she so obsessed with not changing anything?"

"I have no idea. But here's another number for you. Dusty, the Texas Tornado, used to go on last in a bouffant wig and silver veils."

"Can you give me her real name?"

"Yes, I can." I hesitated two beats for dramatic emphasis. "It's Toby Castle."

"What?!" Poor Frank dropped his pen, and it bounced off the table onto the dark sticky floor where he'd probably never find it. Nor did he try. "You don't mean the same Toby Castle who runs the battered-wives hangout?"

Good idea using cheap pens.

"They call it the Domestic Aid Center, for women who need protection from violent men. Yes, that's her operation."

He registered total bewilderment.

"But Castle is a *lesbian,* and a very masculine one at *that.* How could she have worked as a stripper?"

"With a firm body, and great muscle control. Toby did a specialty act with ball-joint tassels." I rotated my index fingers counterclockwise. "She would dip them in lighter fluid, set them on fire, and twirl them in the dark."

Frank nodded. "I remember those fire tassels. But I seem to recall a beautiful blond twirling them around."

"She was only blond for the stage. Under that Lynn Anderson wig, her hair was coal black and cut short as a guy's."

And every night after the show, Toby would put on a three-piece suit, stuff a sock in her pants, and strut out the front door in drag looking just like a man. None of the customers at the bar ever recognized her as the tassel girl.

I said, "Toby always had male vibes."

He said, "I don't doubt it."

Back then when all the "real" men working on the street were rat-faced hustlers without a breath of gentility, Toby was the closest thing we had to a cavalier. She was so generous with Sapphic poetry and courtly manners that a little necking in the ladies' room came to be de rigueur for love-hungry strippers.

Frank was probing the hard drive of his mind, squinting with the effort. "After that, Castle got to be the top female boxer in the region, right?"

I just made a face and said, "Yuck."

Female boxing was a freak show that came and went in the late seventies, to be promptly supplanted by a women's sport with more class, bikini mud wrestling.

He followed the thought. "And I remember no one could beat her."

"Toby retired after only three major fights. Said she couldn't stand to hit a woman."

"Men, though, are fair targets." Frank mock-shuddered. "That woman is more butch than *I* am. And she doesn't let any males near her place. I heard she's got guns, dogs, a whole militia of crazy lesbians over there."

"You can stop sweating." I held up my pen. "Just give me a copy of that photo. I volunteer to beard Ms. Castle in her den and ask all the pertinent questions."

"Thank you, thank you." Displaying a pathetic degree of relief, he pulled a yellow pencil out of his pocket and drew a star on his pad. "Those were all the girls?"

"There weren't only girls working here," I reminded. "Don't forget Ray Lowery, the manager. I hated him."

"What for?"

"He was always shorting the dancers. If a girl was a half hour late for work, he'd dock her four hours' pay."

"Now I get it. Of course *you* couldn't hate anyone that much unless there was money involved."

"And cruelty. The girls who worked for him in the winter said he'd keep the doors wide open even in freezing weather."

"That had to be so the customers could see inside."

"What they would see would be a blue girl in a G-string shivering her butt off. Risking pneumonia just so Ray could make another dollar. He was a real creep. Still is."

"Then he's still around?"

"Right up the street at Le Boucle Restaurant. He sweeps out the place."

"How did Lowery go from club manager to cleanup man?"

"It wasn't that far a trip."

"It would have been for him. Was he a drinker?"

"More like a thief. The club owners on Bourbon always expected *some* stealing and just figured that into the cost of doing business. But they got to losing entirely too much on Madame Julie's. I remember how Ray was working all the angles." I got mad all over again just thinking about the weasel. "He would water the liquor, sell supplies out the back door, skim the take, pad expenses, underring sales . . . The owners finally got fed up and blacklisted him all over town."

"There's a good lead. I'll admit that a man is a more likely suspect than a woman."

"And do you remember our bartender?"

"Hardly. I was always looking over the bartender's head."

"Six feet tall, sturdy build, used to wear ruffled paisley shirts and a teased pompadour like this." I pulled up my hair. "Sealed with a ton of hair spray. His name was Reggie, but he went by Regina."

"A queen built like a football player?"

" 'She' thought of herself as a woman trapped in a football player's body. So, okay, we dancers accepted her as whatever she wanted to be, and she had the run of the dressing room just like the other girls."

"It seemed you dancers were very tolerant of people with alternate lifestyles—so long as they were white."

"Regina was an orphan, sort of. Her parents disowned her when they found out she was gay, so she lived alone in an apartment upstairs."

"Right upstairs? Then she—what am I saying? *He*—might have seen something."

"And I remember one other man who worked here." My Coke was nothing but melted ice now. I moved it to the table behind us. "There was a new guy on the door that month, a kid named Jimmy Turner just back from Nam."

"Maybe the same age as the deceased?" Frank's pencil moved. "They could have been friends."

"But Jimmy never hung out with hippies. He was the straight short-haired type." I leaned forward to give him the capper, sotto voice. "The type who becomes a *lawyer*."

"A lawyer . . ." Then came the dawn, and Frank's pencil stopped. "You're telling me that Jimmy the doorman grew up to be Jim *Turner* the personal injury lawyer?"

"That's the guy. He's gotten to be a big shot."

" 'Shot' isn't the word I'd use."

Before parting company, Frank and I wound down with a

few jokes about lawyers, fair game for all the old gags that used to be anti-ethnic. Lawyers are the new despised minority. Even liberals hate them.

On my way out of the club, I spotted the one decoration that hadn't been there in the old days. Taped to the bar mirror was a photocopied picture of a scowling Saddam Hussein under the handprinted imperative "Wanted Dead or Dead!"

Two

Home for me is the Bywater section of the city's notorious Ninth Ward. I bought myself a big house on Piety Street back in '71, before the real estate boom, bubble, and bust. The place was on the bargain block that year because the neighborhood was considered "going." Blacks had just bought houses on either side, and slumlords were partitioning nearby mansions into multiple dwellings. The middle class had run off to the suburbs for their dream homes of brick and all-white schools for their children.

Years later, in the mid-eighties, a hoard of barren yuppies swarmed into the city and began buying the neglected and run-down multiple dwellings for conversion back into single homes. So for a while my neighborhood was officially "coming back."

But for the last couple of years, since the invention of crack cocaine (with its franchised dealers every two blocks), all the Ninth Ward has been written off as totally "gone."

I had stopped on Frenchman for a copy of *Southern Lavender* magazine and had to hold it in my teeth as I needed both hands to unlock the iron door gate. The solid wood front door required a second key, and then I was inside at last.

"Honey, I'm home!"

"Glad you're back safe, dear."

The man of the house was in our living room ensconced in his recliner and writing on a yellow pad with a fountain pen.

"Yeah, Neg. I amaze myself, every time I make it."

"Modern life."

Julian prefers natural fibers even though they wrinkle. Today he had on a light wool sweater with all-cotton Dockers and looked very casual in a "Pip, pip, tennis anyone?" kind of way.

I put my purse down and dropped the magazine on the coffee table in front of him. "Get a load of this."

Julian picked it up, then opened his hand and let it fall again.

"*Southern Lavender?* You read this rag?"

I pulled off my Easy Spirit shoes and wiggled my toes.

"Why not? Gay magazines have the best gossip."

"The most, the cattiest, but *not* the best."

"This one has a neat column called 'Take Them for an Outing,' where they expose a bunch of southern closet queens."

He stiffened. "That's disgusting, Margo. Whose business is it what a person does in bed or with whom?"

"But these are all public people, Neg. Public hypocrites. Hey, you know Police Chief Yankel, who's been raiding those gay bars in Point Kulm?"

"You don't mean *he* . . . !"

"As a purple dollar."

"I don't believe it."

"*Southern Lavender* wouldn't dare print it if it weren't true." I wriggled out of my panty hose. "Because the guy could sue them."

"He could but he wouldn't." Julian beat the magazine cover with his pen in a rat-tat-tat. "Suing would just call national attention to the charge. Then even if Yankel managed to prove malice and won a law suit, the magazine wouldn't have enough assets even to pay his lawyer, and the public would still be left in doubt about him. 'Where there's smoke, there's fire,' people would say."

"That's what *I* say."

He frowned deeply. "I'm grateful that I'm not important enough to be a target for those trash liners."

"Say, that looks interesting . . . " I wasn't about to change his mind about gay gossip, so diverted him to another subject. "What are you writing there?"

"Another speech on the French Landmark Society."

My distinguished husband spends all his spare time extolling and preserving relics of New Orleans history. His family, the Fortiers, have been members of the local aristocracy since the early 1700s, when this town was nothing but a rustic French settlement.

"Bragging about your decrepit old buildings, huh?"

"It's what I do best."

Julian himself is descended from three generations of second sons of scant ambition, so when I met him there was no money left in his branch of the family. But he still had the Fortier name, and that's worth more than money in New Orleans.

Good jobs in this city tend to be inherited or passed around among the oligarchy. I got on the newspaper only because I became a Fortier. And my husband's uncle went to Jesuit with the brother-in-law of a brother-in-law.

Julian offered this Yankee bar girl the quickest route from the runways of Bourbon Street to the drawing rooms of St. Charles Avenue. I offered him in return a big, comfortable house and the aspect of a heterosexual married man. We offered each other support, partnership, and great conversation.

The Julian Fortiers have been thriving and prospering under this arrangement for fifteen years.

I sat on the floor and stretched out my legs to keep the old jogging muscles from cramping up.

"I had this great dream that I was dancing with Alexander Godunov."

"You, dancing? Ha!"

"Well, actually he was holding me up over his head in his deliciously strong arms."

"Which broke?"

"No, I was light as a feather, like Gelsey Kirkland in her prime. Then slowly, Alexander lifted me down till I was on-point."

"Of head?"

"No, of my little feet."

"Little?!"

"Well, they were size five in the dream. Then he gathered me into his sinewy, muscular arms."

"Then what happened?"

"Nothing, dammit. Then the cruddy phone rang and I woke up."

"Was it Godunov, at least?"

"Hardly such luck. It was just Frank Washington."

I brought my head to my right knee, carefully so as not to rip a tendon. "Who are you propagandizing now?"

"This is for an assembly at Warren Easton."

"You're going to waste another of your stirring speeches on high school kids?"

"Who is more important than high school kids?" He made a margin note. "If we can just instill them with some pride in their past, maybe they'll have more confidence in their future."

"A Christian sentiment, but how are you going to get modern, fast-rapping, five-slapping, moon-walking kids to look at slides of old houses?"

"They'll be interested to know their own ancestors built those old houses and lived and died in them."

I bent all the way over and touched my forehead to the rug.

"They'd be more interested if *Michael Jackson's* ancestors lived in those houses."

"Real history is more compelling than any action video." Julian recapped his Mont Blanc. "Goodness, Margo. Do you have to twist yourself into a pretzel like that?"

"I'm just staying fit for sex," I grunted to the rug pile. "Men like a woman to be supple."

"What men? Don't flatter yourself."

"Mmf. I'll admit that I haven't been involved with anyone in a while."

"Quite a long while, my dear."

"But I'll meet someone nice pretty soon."

"I sincerely hope so, but . . . " He leaned forward in his chair till his head was right above mine. "You know, men aren't attracted to women who are so pitifully *desperate*."

"Hey, I don't look desperate—mmf—I always dress in a modest ladylike fashion."

"Seemingly, love. But underneath that modest ladylike dress, you pulsate with the vibrations of some enormous vaginal *vortex* that just sucks up anything within range!"

"So what do you expect? I'm forty-five years old, in my sexual prime."

He straightened up then and went back to his speech. "Why would anyone want a woman in her sexual prime?"

"Maybe because we try harder." I sat upright with a painful "Ugh!" and pulled my legs together manually. "When I was twenty years old with no education, and no connections, I had to become a professional bimbo just to make ends meet."

"So I've heard." Julian used his pen precipitously to dot an *i* or cross a *t*. "You've come a long way since then."

"Not so long." I turned over on all fours for leverage and climbed to my feet. "What's a gossip columnist, after all? Nothing more than the bimbo of journalism."

"So now you have the education *and* the connections. What do you want to be?"

"I want to be respected as a reporter." I lurched on painfully stretched muscles over to my purse for the crime scene photo, then lurched back again to sit on the arm of Julian's chair. "This is my ticket to the majors." And I told him everything I knew about the hippie in the wall, which took all of two minutes.

"So?" He studied the picture, then lay it down, facedown. "Now you see yourself as a sort of shopworn Brenda Starr?"

"Just think! If I can make good with this story, I might graduate from gossip into hard news."

"Pulitzer country."

"That's my dream."

He patted my shoulder. "And a worthy one it is, dear. If there's any way I can help, I sit ready."

"Maybe you can." I shifted my behind over to the coffee table. "Tell me what you remember about 1970."

"In 1970 . . ." Julian sat back in his recliner and gazed up at the crystal chandelier for inspiration. ". . . I was twenty years old and colors were brighter, I seem to recall."

"That's because we all wore psychedelics and Pucci back then. Before beige was invented."

"And there were no shadows either because our faces were flat, bland, and unwrinkled."

"We girls went nowhere without big floppy eyelashes. All anyone could see of me in those days was my Maybelline. Did you ever make the Bourbon Street scene?"

"Not I. Nineteen seventy was my junior year abroad, so I spent most of it in France." He tapped his pen. "I remember that General de Gaulle died that year. And the peace talks were going on in Paris, but there was no peace, of course—then as now. *Le plus ça change . . .* "

" 'The more it changes, the more it remains the same.' But not me. You know, I don't feel as though I've changed at all. Hey!" I clapped my hands with an inspiration. "I've got a fun idea, Julian. Let's just turn the lights down low, sit on the floor, and listen to my old *Hair* album."

"Gracious, is that thing still around?"

"Sure. The record's pretty scratchy by now, but it still plays 'Aquarius' and 'Good Morning Starshine.' So I'll get us some Chianti we can drink right out of the bottle, and maybe there's even some incense around to burn in an ashtray. How about it?"

He considered the suggestion a moment, but then shook his head firmly.

"Margo dear, I haven't sat on the floor in ten years. My legs don't bend that way anymore. Cheap wine brings on my allergies, and that smelly incense would only stick in the curtains for weeks. Besides, I want to tune in CNN and check up on the war."

"Okay. Sure."

Welcome to 1991.

THREE

February 14, 1991

I hate driving down to the paper. Most days, I simply write the column at home and transmit it to my editor, Felix Dune, via the wonder of the fax machine. But this afternoon, I had to talk to Felix, convince Felix, in person. So it was mine to make my way through his cluttered mess of an office, past the ubiquitous cartoon of the "Iraqi Missile Launcher" taped to a filing cabinet, Felix's idea of manifest wit.

The crude line drawing of the hapless camel with a missile in his mouth and his groin about to be banged with a mallet was faxed all over the country in one morning, early last week.

I dropped my hard copy on the desk.

"Here's tomorrow's column about the Cabildo." I lightened my voice to do "perky" and bounced in my shoes. "I hope you like it."

"What the hell does it matter if *I* like it?" He clenched his cigarette between his teeth and spoke around it. "The *readers* like it. The *advertisers* like it, so the *accountants* like it."

"Thank you."

"This place is a madhouse today." He slapped the stack of papers in his Out box. "I edited five stories about the war since lunch."

"It's a winning topic. Jay Leno says Hussein already used up half his ammunition just executing his own generals."

"That's funny." My editor felt around his desk for an ashtray, moving stacks of paper aside. "It'll probably make a sidebar."

"Is the paper pro or con?"

"You kidding? Wars sell papers."

"So said William Randolph Hearst or Orson Welles or someone."

Felix finally located an ashtray under his Yellow Pages. "I didn't like Bush before, but now I'm getting to admire him for what he's doing."

"What? Starting a fight? What's that cost him?"

"You have to credit the guy in one way. He leaves the strategy to the generals, not like Kennedy and Johnson."

"At least those two kept our collective ass out of the Middle East. Oil isn't worth fighting for."

Felix yawned, and his dry throat rattled. "There's nothing the hell else over there."

"That's *your* redneck opinion." I leaned across his desk. "One's overview of the Middle East situation hinges on whether one basically likes Jews or basically doesn't."

"I'm neutral."

"You can't be neutral."

"Well, I am because I don't like Arabs either."

I took umbrage and a chair. "I always believed that the Jews were God's Chosen People and Israel was their Promised Land."

"You read Bible stories in grammar school."

"No, I read *Exodus* in high school."

I had only been in there two minutes and was already blinking from the smoke and wondering why it never bothered Felix. Then he went into a coughing fit.

"So, Margo?" Cough. "What's up?" my esteemed editor queried on his way to the rattling window. He threw it open and stuck his head outside, then coughed again.

"I need a week off from the column," I told his rear end.

"What the"—cough—"hell for?"

"I'm into a fantastic story. A twenty-one-year-old murder on Bourbon Street that's still unsolved."

"Tell you what, Margo." Felix came back through the window. "People are murdered in this city every day. 'Give me your drugs, bang-bang, you're dead.' A lot of them"—cough—"go unsolved and nobody much cares. Not like they care about Zella Funck's scandalous new art show. *That's* what you should be working on."

"Just take a look here." I held out the photograph of the skeleton. "This should make the lead in the Sunday Pictorial."

"What in hell . . . ?" He lowered himself into his groaning desk chair and accepted the picture. "Who was he?"

"We don't know yet."

"Yeah? Well, there's no story here unless we ferret out the who and why."

"I expect to. Lieutenant Frank Washington is letting me work on the case with him."

"Never mind." Felix snapped his fingers against the photo. "If the story is that good, we'll let Barney handle it. He's our police reporter, remember? You stick to what you're good at, which is society."

"But Frank doesn't *want* Barney. He's asked specifically to work with *me*."

"What in hell for?"

"Because . . . " (Think fast.) "He says *I* would be better at questioning the people involved in the case. He knows I'm the sensitive type."

"You 'sensitive'?" Felix snorted. "This is the first *I've* heard about it. Okay." He shook the photo down like a thermometer. "I'll put Millie on the column for a week. But if you don't make this a feature, that week comes off your vacation time."

"You're a mensch, Felix."

"What's that?"

"It doesn't matter. I meant it sarcastically."

Four

I tooled down Canal Street on my way across town and turned right at Simon Bolivar Square, where a demonstration was in progress. A ring of slow-walking picketers toted posters lettered with Marks-A-Lots.

NO BLOOD FOR OIL! the pasteboards proclaimed, and STAY OUT OF THE WAR!

"Hell, no! We won't go!" the protesters droned in tired unison. "We won't fight for Texaco!"

Some of the advocates were gray and fat and bearded, looking like leftovers from the last round of antiwar demonstrations. Perhaps they still had a few good chants left in them, so they just made fresh signs.

But this contingent represents a minority opinion in New Orleans today. Most of my townsmen are leaping at the opportunity to wave the flag, beat the drum, and "Stand for something!"

Last year, the parade Krewe of Endymion had booked Woody Harrelson from the TV show "Cheers" to be their king at Mardi Gras. But when the actor was shown on the news protesting Desert Storm, the good Americans of Endymion started hollering that he was a traitor to our brave warriors in the Middle East and, gol' darn it, they didn't want him for their king after all. Harrelson called a press conference to explain that it wasn't the *soldiers* he didn't like, it was the *war*. But naturally nobody accepted *that* excuse; anyone who *really* likes soldiers would want to send them *all* off to war *all* the time.

So Harrelson was firmly disinvited, and Endymion stocked the king's float with Police Chief Woodfork and a platoon of uniformed GIs to present the most hawkish contingent possible.

My next stop was a three-story Victorian mansion in the Faubourg Tremé. Through a need for security, there was no sign designating it the Domestic Aid Center. Also the building was enclosed by a twelve-foot iron fence lest any murderous estranged mate get word of its location. Then, for good measure, two brindle boxers stood guard in the front yard. Bitches, of course.

I parked in front (guided into position by the scrape of my fender against the curb), hied up to the locked gate, and rang the bell twice. Then I watched as the big door of carved mahogany opened, and its frame was filled solid with the hulking form of the resident bouncer, who lumbered across the porch and down the steps to challenge me.

The guardian of the door weighed in at two hundred and fifty easy, complete with blue chambray work shirt, khaki pants, and trucker's wallet attached to the belt with a chain. And turquoise earrings.

"Hi, Elizabeth," I said cheerily. "Toby is expecting me."

"Ugh."

Elizabeth detached a ring of keys from her left rear belt loop and used the largest of them on the gate, which opened with a clank and a scrape of the sidewalk as I walked through it. She made no further comment, having used up her conversation with the "Ugh."

Elizabeth is the silent type and not in much social demand.

But if I were running from a violent husband, I would feel absolutely secure in her massive presence. Make that a whole truckload of violent husbands.

In the tiled foyer, a young black woman with a blacker eye knelt on the floor vigorously scrubbing the mosaic Venus sign with soap and ammonia. She looked up at me with suspicion in the good eye. "Yeah?"

"Ms. Castle's office? She's expecting me."

"Down the hall," and back to scrubbing.

I passed the front room, where two little girls sat on a dilapidated sofa playing Monopoly and giggling and bouncing on worn springs whenever the dice were thrown. A k. d. lang album was playing somewhere in back of the house. I didn't see any stereo or speakers but just heard the pure vocals lightly bouncing off the high ceilings and playing with my hair.

"Trail of broken hearts, looking back at you . . ."

At the end of the hallway, Toby's office door was open, and I led with my head, poking it in. "Hello?"

She was cocked back behind her enormous desk, reading a fan-feed report and puffing a panatela. Her hair had grayed since I'd last seen her, but she was still . . . well . . . handsome.

"Oh, hi! I've been waiting for you!"

Toby Castle rose to her full height, a man's height, and moved around to the front of her desk. She was dressed to swash and buckle in black tailored slacks, riding boots, and a man's shirt of ecru satin and put her hand out to take mine, the way men do.

"It's been much too long, Cherry."

I consider shaking hands to be a masculine custom and inappropriate for women, but I gave up mine out of politeness. Then Toby just held it in both of hers and bowed over it as a gallant would with an old mistress. "Or should I call you Mrs. Fortier?"

"Margo is good."

I breathed in her cologne, which was my favorite men's fragrance, V.O., and noticed again the scar on her chin. I had been present the night she'd earned it over at Papa Joe's. A sailor had copped a feel from the girl Toby was escorting, and fisticuffs ensued. I'd put a bet down on Toby and won myself a night's pay.

"Come take the tour; I'll show you around the place." She abandoned the cigar and steered me out the door and back down the hallway. "The *Times-Picayune* did an article on our center just two months ago."

"I read it. I've been following your work closely."

"Then you know what we're about."

"Sure. You're running a refuge for women."

"More than that, Margo. This is a *fortress* for women. No males may intrude, even to make deliveries. We'll launch our revolution from here."

"Revolution?"

"To end the greed and violence brought about by the patriarchy. We're going to change all that."

"You're going to change human nature?"

"*Inhuman* nature. I'm talking about man's basic inhumanity." She took my hand protectively, and I was reluctant to draw away for mixed reasons. "They give us rape, forced motherhood, slavery, mutilation, and these senseless wars over oil and real estate." Her eyes flashed. "Have you ever wondered why *they're* the ones in control? *We* outnumber them."

"They're stronger and more aggressive."

"Useful traits in prehistory, obsolete now."

"They make more money."

"Very true. But why is that, when women naturally work harder and do most jobs better? No, Margo. Male rule will inevitably go the way of the dinosaur."

"Men are a lot of trouble all right. Too bad we can't live without them." Naively, I expected that statement to go uncontested.

"But we *can* live without them, don't you see?" Toby

squeezed my hand. "With cloning technology we women will soon be able to reproduce by ourselves."

"What a dreadful idea."

"Ha!" She emitted a one-syllable laugh. "You'll come into the fold once you see the whole picture." She stopped and opened the door to a well-lighted oval room with bay windows. "This is our strategy room."

The "strategy room" was painted pink and white with bright red accents. A very normal-looking group of women sat around on floor cushions chatting and painting posters. The TV was on and tuned to CNN, as they all are these days, but nobody was watching Charles Jaco report from the roof of the Riyadh Hotel.

"We're getting ready for the Presidents' Day rally," Toby explained. "This is just the first stage of our campaign." She picked up a poster depicting a red fist inside a silver Venus sign. "We women have the numbers; we have the interest. But the male establishment still makes the laws. Vera over there is an example of what we're up against."

She indicated a woman who squatted on the floor trying to interest a toddler in a stuffed bunny. Vera bounced the bunny around and talked for it, but the child, a boy in blue overalls with green bruises on his arms, seemed to see nothing.

"Her ex-husband was beating up on poor little Jonathan," Toby said. "But would you believe that Michigan judge gave *him* custody?"

"I believe I'd want to know why."

"Sexual politics, what else? In a patriarchal society, a man's home is his castle and his family his property, insulated from the law. So Vera had no recourse but to pick up the kid on a visiting day, leave everything behind, and run with him."

"Isn't that legally child stealing?"

"It's called 'defiance of a custody order,' but, yes, she is breaking the law. And so did everyone along the route who offered her a safe house."

"I've read about those hiding places. They claim to be analogous to the Underground Railroad that smuggled slaves up to the free North."

Toby set her jaw. "They're women and men who are concerned enough with a child's welfare to risk prison terms."

"The trick is in finding out what the child's welfare really is." I lowered my voice. "When was Jonathan taken away from his abusive father in Michigan?"

"Oh . . . " She looked puzzled. "About five days ago. Why?"

"Those bruises on his arms are more recent than that. Check it out."

"Don't worry, I will."

Last year, child abuse was the sexy issue, to be discussed at length on every chairs-in-a-row talk show and rating covers on all the major magazines. Legislators up for reelection beat their drums for protective bills and appropriations.

This year, of course, the time and ink have been diverted to the war and so will follow the appropriations. The kids can go blow.

Toby was still talking, and I tuned her back in.

" . . . Women can take the power away from the men next November if only we unify behind one strong feminist candidate."

"Some men who hold office now are feminists."

"Men?!" Her voice rose. "It's up to *women* to take care of women. There's another case." Toby pointed with her scarred chin to a pregnant young brunette. "Jenny Redbird."

Jenny Redbird had removed herself from the group and was engrossed in a supermarket tabloid bannering Roseanne Barr's enduring passion for Tom Arnold. "She's a full-blooded Native American with inherited alcoholism. Her first child inherited F.A.S."

"Fetal alcohol syndrome?"

"Right. The poor kid is hopelessly retarded and in foster

care for life. Now Jenny's pregnant again, and she knows she couldn't keep herself from drinking out there." My host waved at the cold "man's world" outside the window. "So she's come to stay with us, and we'll take care of all her needs till the baby is born."

"Then what?"

"Then we'll have a whole baby."

"But meanwhile . . . " I stepped close enough to speak into her ear. "Any time Ms. Redbird gets thirsty, she can walk right out the door and start drinking again."

"Yes." Toby led me out of the strategy room and shut the door behind us.

"Unfortunately, that's the flaw in the plan."

Back in the privacy of her office, I settled on the tufted leather couch before asking, "What will you do if the girl decides to leave?"

Toby resumed her seat and tilted it back.

"What would you suggest?"

"I'd keep her locked up till the kid is born."

"False imprisonment. You want to abrogate her civil rights?"

"What about the baby's right not to be mentally crippled?"

"If you start promoting fetal rights above the mothers', you're getting into bed with those antichoice lunatics."

"Once a woman chooses to have a baby," I said, "it should be called a person and protected under the law."

"In some areas it is. Women have already been indicted for passing an illegal substance to a minor, meaning their own unborn children. But alcohol is a legal substance."

"No less harmful."

"Sure, alcohol is harmful to a fetus, but so is tobacco." Toby picked up her cigar again and relit it, drawing deep puffs. "And maybe coffee, too. What about horseback riding, scuba diving . . . You want to lock up every pregnant woman? How about any woman who *might* be pregnant?"

31

"I wouldn't take it that far."

"Once it goes, Margo, *you* don't get to choose how far it's taken."

"How many defective babies can this society support?"

"I'm afraid we're going to find out."

Toby looked up and watched her cigar smoke a minute before saying, "Now you know my agenda. What's yours?"

I opened my purse and took out the fatal photograph. "We're trying to identify some human remains. It's rather ugly."

She put down the cigar to accept the picture and regarded it coolly without attempting to cover the skull face. After a moment she handed it back. "Where did you find him?"

"He was sealed into the wall at Madame Julie's in June of '70."

"If that had happened in front of me, I would have said something."

"I'm sure, but if you saw him around while he was still alive, you might remember the hair and the clothes."

"Not likely. I've never looked too closely at men. They don't interest me."

"Suppose he came into the club to watch your act, gave you a tip, offered you a drink . . . "

"If he had, I wouldn't have noticed. I didn't see the customers when I was working. I always liked to fantasize a house packed with luscious women."

"If you recall anything about him, please let me know."

She picked up the cigar again. "I won't—why don't you ask your society friend?"

"She's on the list. I'm going to talk to all the other dancers."

"All of them?" Toby smiled, and there was a rare softness in her eyes. "When you see Sheila Casey, give her my best."

"You remember Sheila?"

"Who wouldn't? . . . She was the most beautiful girl who

ever walked the earth. Like an orchid, an exquisite flower who had to be protected from the elements."

I was alerted. "What makes you say that? Did you ever feel a need to protect her?"

She drew back. "Anyone would. The poor child was an innocent, easily fooled."

That's all I was going to get out of Toby Castle today. I stood up and gave her my hand again and again felt those old macho vibes.

"Thank you for seeing me."

She rose and smiled down at me. "Thank you for the sight." And she escorted me down the hall with one hand lightly on my shoulder.

As we reached the front door, I stopped and spoke into her ear. "Say . . . can you still twirl those fire tassels?"

"Only for lovers. Want to see?"

"It would be interesting."

Five

Next on my list of interviewees was Jim Turner the lawyer, formerly Jimmy the doorman. I wanted to get him over with.

So where does one find the most famous personal injury lawyer in New Orleans? Well, certainly not in his office, much less in a courtroom. Today he was doing his *real* work at the Lake Shore Levee. I parked my car on the shoulder and climbed over a DO NOT ENTER sign to reach his mini–production company.

The video camera was set on a tripod and turned toward the lake to frame the subject with a rugged, outdoor background.

I recognized the director, Paul Wynn, as the highest paid commercial producer in the area, renowned for making twerps look like dynamos. Today he had his work cut out for him.

Jim Turner, Esq., wore a lawyerly Brooks Brothers suit with a yellow ribbon as a boutonniere. He glowered into the camera till his cue of a shot finger, at which he exploded into a friendly grin.

"Have an accident?! Hurt on the job?! *Who* do you turn to? Call *me*, Jim Turner."

He used to show the same hustle back when he was working the door.

"Show time!" he would crow to tourists passing by. "Sweet *Cherry* coming up next. Watch how she shakes that thing." He would open the door quickly for a teasing glimpse of girl flesh, then shut it again. "Buy one drink; see the entire show! No cover, no *nothing!*"

Twenty-one years later, the barker's delivery hadn't changed.

"Come in tomorrow for your free consultation! I'll tell *you* what your rights are!" And he pointed to the video camera, smirking the smirk of the triumphant.

I elbowed Paul Wynn. "Know what's the difference between a truckload of bowling balls and a truckload of dead lawyers?"

"You can't unload bowling balls with a pitchfork," he said to me only. "Now for the fifteen-second version!" he called to everyone else.

A plump young hausfrau was moved to her mark as though on wheels. As the camera rolled, she held up a fan of ten-dollar bills and screeched, "I called Jim Turner and got *my* money in two months!"

She was followed onstage by a middle-aged man who looked like Daryl or Daryl and brandished the same prop.

"Jim Turner got me mine in *six weeks!*" he assured his friends in Television Land.

The subject of these glowing endorsements backed into a director's chair stenciled with his name while a jean-clad woman got busy applying a rattail comb to his moussed hairdo.

That's when I moved in. "Hi, Jim."

"Hi! How are you?" He smiled automatically and stuck out his paw. Then he did a take and squinted. "Aren't you that columnist?" He snapped his fingers. "Margo Fortier! I read you every day."

"Do tell. I tried to see you at your office, but it seems you're hardly ever there."

"Nah. I usually let my people handle the office." He beckoned for the mirror and held it at arm's length to check his makeup. "You want to interview me?" He stroked his strong cleft chin. "I have a real success story to tell."

I'd never noticed any such chin back in 1970. He might have sprung for a John DeLorean–style implant.

"No doubt. Would it start with your early days on Bourbon Street?"

"Yeah!" He sniggered. "When I first hit town I was just back from Nam, had no connections. I was lucky to get a job as a doorman for one of the girlie shows."

"Madame Julie's"

That startled him so much that he almost took his eyes from the mirror. "How do *you* know?"

"I was one of the girlies."

"Hah! Then let's just make a pact." He winked. "You don't tell on me, and I won't tell on you."

"I swear that nothing you tell me now is for publication."

"Fair enough."

"I seem to remember your hair was lighter twenty years ago."

"Streaked." He patted it gently. "Chicks went for the surfer look back then. But I commissioned a survey on hair color and found out brown inspires more trust." He assessed his reflection, swiveling from right to left. "With just a *touch* of gray at the temples. Some people have told me I look like Alec Baldwin. What do you think?"

"Don't invest with them." I pulled the coroner's picture from my purse. "I've got something unpleasant to show you."

Turner put the mirror down, carefully, so as not to smudge the glass. "Just so this isn't a bill," he chortled, then took the picture for a close look. "Oh God!" He turned gratifyingly white and handed it back with shaking fingers. "Wh . . . what's that? A still from a horror movie?"

"The poor soul was sealed into a wall at Madame Julie's in June of '70, while you and I were working there."

"You mean we had a murderer stalking around all that time?" He shuddered. "Hell, I saw enough of death in the war."

"Your distinguished service record has been well publicized."

"Those VFW guys like to make a big deal out of it."

"Maybe because of your generous donations every year."

He winked again. "Networking is important in my line. Everybody I meet knows someone who knows someone else."

"How friendly."

"Say, going with that . . . " Turner spoke out of the side of his mouth as though that would prevent anyone else from hearing. "If you could bring me some business from those old money friends of yours, there'd be a nice finder's fee in it for you."

I thought, "Fuck *this* asshole," and said, "I'll certainly keep that in mind."

Six

I parked my car by the Jax Brewery, then stood out on the Moon Walk to watch orange clouds in the blue sky turn shocking pink, then purple, then smoky gray as the sun set all along the Mississippi.

By then it was five-thirty, according to my practical Omega watch, and time to touch base with my new partner. Onward and upward.

The redoubtable lieutenant was waiting for me at the French Market café and had already ordered us a plateful of hot beignets, coffee for himself, and chocolate milk for me. I plomped into the chair opposite his and placed my purse, pad, and two pens on the table between us. Frank's pad and pen were already there. Now we had done all we could, short of hoisting a sign, to indicate that this was a business meeting and not an interracial date.

If you want to venture a hazardous meal in New Orleans, try being a white woman dining with a black man and served by a black waitress. Everything that can possibly go wrong at that table *will* go wrong. Guaranteed.

"Oh, you wanted it *rare?* I thought you said very well-done . . . That's okay, miss. This dress is washable . . . Why is the beer warm? . . . Is potato soup supposed to have bones?"

And all the time she's ruining your meal, the waitress will play absolutely dumb, never giving away by word or gesture her profound disgust at the soul brother who's out making time with this white bitch.

I picked up my straw and daintily blew the paper off.

"I interviewed Toby Castle."

"And, wait, let me guess." Frank used his napkin to brush powdered sugar from his mustache. "She knows nothing, right?"

"Wrong. She knows women should rule the world and we don't need you guys at all."

"So you got an idea why I wasn't craving to swim her moat."

"I also got an education in feminist social science, but zilch on the hippie in the wall." Then I hit the beignets, which were hot and golden brown, and demolished two before continuing my report. "Next I talked to Jim Turner while he posed for a commercial out on the levee."

"Is he still out there? I may pray for a tidal wave."

"Why do you sound so personal? He's nothing but your generic ambulance chaser."

"He also chases police cars." Frank made two fists and laid them on the table. "Turner has sued the department three times for injuries that occurred to criminals in custody."

My hand stole back to the plate. "Just sort of 'occurred' like an act of God?"

He tightened the fists. "When a two-hundred-pound armed robber works his handcuffs down over his hips and around and then tries to strangle a policewoman with them, it doesn't take divine intervention to make things 'occur.' "

"So there were extenuating circumstances, but someone has to be custodying the custodiat." I took a bite of warm beignet, then a sip of cold chocolate, alternating the two tastes. "Turner calls himself a 'champion of the poor.' He claims he's willing to take on the establishment in his fight for truth and justice."

"Justice was never his agenda. Turner will sue anyone with deep pockets, and his favorite target is the taxpaying public." The indignant man of the law left a dollar under his cup. "Would you like me to order more doughnuts?"

"No, five is enough. I'm not a big eater." I rolled the last one in the loose sugar on the plate. "How can we go looking under suspects for motives when we still have no idea who the victim was?"

"There's a way to find out what he looked like." Frank gazed past me, at a mule-drawn carriage clop-clopping down Decatur Street. "A forensic sculptor can reconstruct the hippie's face from his skull. I've already contacted Tulane Medical Center."

"How long will that take?"

"Only a few days. I've made it a priority."

He pulled a glassine bag from his breast pocket and rubbed the contents with his thumb as though it were a talisman.

I reached across the table and took it from his hand, a silver pendant on a chain. "I never see these anymore."

Frank nodded. "That was the hippie's peace medal. I've forgotten the significance of the symbol, if I ever knew."

"N.D. for Nuclear Disarmament. That's what it meant."

I held my hand up with the first and second fingers forming a V. When Winston Churchill made the gesture, it meant "Victory." But when Dave Garroway did the same on the original "Today" show (before Deborah Norville was even born) it meant "Peace."

"So where to next, Frank? I presume you'll be hitting all the Bourbon Street bars interviewing old-timers. Or maybe you'll be spending the night in the police lab, studying dust with a microscope."

"Wrong again, Whatsit. At this point, I'm just going to drive home, fall into my easy chair, and watch the war."

Seven

I had a date to meet my best friend, Gaby Schindler, in the Windsor Court Hotel at exactly six-thirty, and we were both exactly on time. I out of respect and she because she's a German and they're exact about everything.

I helped her off with her coat. "How was your trip?"

"Ach, Budapest vas depressing." She lowered herself into her chair, bracing on the armrests.

Gaby is a baroness, epicure, polyglot, and veteran of the Berlin underground during the Reich. "It vas so shabby, just like a city after the vhar. Der vas nothing in the shops to buy." She shook her head in slow motion. "Und it vas such a delightful place last time I vas dere."

I folded the coat and gave it the third place at our table.

"That was before the Communists, right?"

"Before eeffen the Nazis."

She had just turned seventy-seven, but in a lot of ways Gaby is younger than I. She travels all over the world at "golden agers'" rates, taking off at a moment's notice and trekking through war zones and police states with less thought than I would give to a run to Schwegmann's. Here in a small town like New Orleans, there aren't too many people I find scintillating, and I feel an affinity with her European chic and sophistication.

Or more probably there isn't the teensiest bit of affinity between us but she just represents what I'd *like* to be. So the cultivated baroness has served as my exemplar for the "Lady" bit as well as my enthusiastic partner in adventure since we first met at an art gallery some ten years ago.

(I had attended because I wanted to get it on with a patron of the gallery. Gaby was actually interested in the paintings.)

In another sense, I'm running around playing "Margie Albright" and Gaby is my "Mrs. Odetts."

This evening we were having high tea in "La Salle." Only it wasn't tea for me, it was a Coke, and it wasn't tea for her, either, it was white wine. But the proper cakes were served, hotly and deliciously.

She began by buttering a scone.

"Vhat haff you been doing, dear?"

"I'm trying to get some respect over at the newspaper."

"Respect?" Gracefully, she let her napkin fall open and draped it in her lap.

"Just *some*. I don't have a smidgen of it now. Next to *me*, Rodney Dangerfield is *worshiped*." I executed the same trick with my own napkin. "So I'm helping Lieutenant Washington solve the murder of a twenty-one-year-old skeleton and interviewing former strippers. But nothing interesting is going on."

Gaby gave a delicate wave of her scone. "Vhen you say nutting interesting, you mean only that you don't haff a lover now."

"Now? Cripe! It's been so long since I've kissed anyone, I think my tongue is frozen in the retracted position." I knocked a miniature cream puff off the plate and had to put it back.

"This is an unnatural state of being, Gaby. Where are all the virile men?"

"Margo, you alvays carry on so about dis. But vhy is it such an important t'ing?" She flicked a hand, and her heirloom ring glinted in emerald green. "Luff is important for happiness, yes."

"No shi—kidding."

"But does it haf to be a *man?*"

"What else is there?"

"Lot's of t'ings . . . " She looked at her ring for guidance, then came up with, "You could perhaps adopt a *child.*"

"Yuk."

"Vell, I don't like dem either." She wrinkled her patrician nose. "So noisy and vhet. But surely you don't vant to give up your life vit' Julian and run avay on some adventure?"

"Of course not. Julian and I get along great. There just isn't any sex involved."

"Den why the difficulty?" She looked around carefully and lowered her voice to a whisper. "Dis is a *port* town, Margo. If you vould simply like to haff a fling, you can pick up some handsome young Nordic seaman and enjoy all de sex you like all night long."

"That's no good." I hissed back at her. "I couldn't get interested in some kid. I need a man of *substance.* Someone I can *dedicate* myself to."

"So-oo?" She considered that while tearing a croissant. "You vish to get deeply involfed in a superficial affair."

"Yeah."

"Ah."

"See, I never *plan* for it to happen. I just fall hard for some guy, waste most of my time pacing around the rug, waiting for him to call, shopping for clothes he would like, making myself stunning for him, daydreaming about him . . . " I waved my chocolate truffle distractedly. "It uses up all my emotional energy. Then I can't function. My work goes to pieces."

"I t'ink you allow yourself to become *too* involfed."

"One month I'm ready to *die* for the guy, then he disappoints me in some terminal way and—bang!—it's all over." I broke the chocolate truffle into jagged halves. "Then I get to feeling badly ripped off and start wishing *he* would drop dead. After that I spend the next six months just stumbling around muttering to myself."

"Until de next vun comes along und den you start all ofer."

"Gaby, I don't know why I would even consider going through all that again. Relationships take so much out of me."

"I t'ink you enjoy enacting dese little dramas."

"Though practically speaking . . . " I started in on the truffle, taking a little tiny bite. "I think I *should* have another affair just for health reasons."

"For health reasons?"

"Absolutely. During menopause a woman *needs* to stay sexually active to keep the hormones flowing. Or else she'll dry up and get heart disease and osteoporosis. I can't let *that* happen, can I?"

"No, certainly not. But Margo . . . " Gaby leaned across the table and put her hand on mine. "My dear, you must try not to look so desperate."

Eight

"Evening, Miz Fortier." The night security guard at the paper touched his cap.

Since I devote serious energy to staying away from the building, I'd never clapped eyes on the man before.

"How did you know it was me?"

"Easy. I recognized you from the photograph on top of that column of yours."

"Cripe. If the photo looks *that* bad, I'm getting a new one taken."

I rode the elevator upstairs to the morgue, where I flipped on the microfilm reader and loaded up the *T-P* for the second week of June 1970, including advertising pages. I pressed down the switch to fast rewind past the classifieds, and before long the dizzying rush of print was making my eyes careen around the inside of my head like pool balls. I stopped it at page one and bent over the lighted screen.

I scanned every column in the ambitious hope of finding a headline like TOURIST DISAPPEARS over an article furnishing name, address, and photo of somebody's missing son or brother.

On June 11 of 1970, Soviet Premier Kosygin was accusing President Nixon of trying to dictate to Indochina.

Six American GIs had just been killed fighting inside Cambodia, where the "key port of Kompong Som was being threatened."

An editorial cartoon avowed that the proposed one-percent raise of our five-percent city sales tax "would add up to torture."

(Now we've got nine and a half percent. Bless us and save us.)

When I got to the TV listings, they looked meager, even primitive. It was a simpler time before cable. You had a choice among four VHF channels, take or leave them.

Dean Martin's guests that evening were to be Ann-Margret and Bob Newhart.

Archie and Jughead went to a roller-skating party.

In Northampton, Massachusetts, a twenty-year-old Amherst college sophomore was sentenced to a hundred-dollar fine and a year in jail for "contemptuous use of the American flag."

"Robert Kingman was arrested in the Hadley shopping area after police received telephone complaints that he was wearing the flag sewn to the seat of his walking shorts."

(Only a year in stir? The judge must have been a bleeding-heart liberal.)

There were several topical articles and ads with prices that made my jaw sag. But, in that edition at least, there was not a single line about a missing youth.

It was past two A.M. by the time I got home to Piety Street. Fortunately, there was a space of about three car lengths right in front of the house, so I didn't have to wake Julian up to come out and parallel park me.

Once inside my front door, I had fifty seconds to turn off the security alarm. If ever it isn't deactivated in time, I will get a phone call from the guard station. Then if I don't answer with my password *(Love)*, a minimum of four uniformed private cops are supposed to come screeching up the block with guns drawn, surround the place, and rescue me from murderous intruders. Theoretically.

I'm not taking these precautions against my black next-door neighbors. It's the ones passing by that I'm scared of.

Julian is always in his room, sound asleep, by this time, so I moved quietly not to disturb him. I kicked off my shoes then, hardly inured to the great national pastime, I grabbed the remote and punched on the TV for the latest Gulf talk.

Bill Moyers had expressed our collective sentiment when he spoke of "the sheer fortifying exhilaration of watching the first live war televised back to our living rooms."

Was Vietnam so long ago? The fighting in Indochina seemed far removed from our lives at the time. Twenty years ago, we would see week-old film footage of field maneuvers on the six o'clock news. They would mainly show uniformed men running around with guns and throwing themselves down in the mud. Sometimes they would be carrying wounded men on stretchers, who would be out of danger or beyond danger by the time their pictures made it to Cronkite's news.

Today, through the magic of satellites, we see and hear correspondents broadcasting live while the air raid sirens whistle around them.

It was fun to watch the French bombardier get his target in the crosshairs, then catch the darkening puff of smoke that indicated a hit. Bingo! Through the mechanism of the SLAM missile's nose camera, we actually get to see an explosion from point zero.

A. Whitney Brown calls this a "Nintendo War."

During the first few days of Desert Storm, I thought we could have ourselves a *fun* war. We could all watch in the comfort of our living rooms as military machinery destroyed other military machinery and not people. In and out; nobody gets hurt.

Then one night CNN spoiled it for me by showing a Saudi

fighter pilot (an Arab on *our* side) being slapped on the back by his buddies and congratulated for shooting down two Iraqi planes (Arabs on *their* side).

"He was the first fighter pilot in this action to get two *kills*," trumpeted the voice-over.

And I sort of wished they'd said two "hits" instead of two "kills." That would make the maneuver seem merely a benign target practice.

I'd rather think about crosshairs on a screen and a nifty puff of smoke than a fearful brown-eyed woman waiting by her door for a husband who would never come home again. Or children crying, "Where's Daddy? He promised he'd read to us tonight."

I had tuned into "CBS Nightwatch" hoping to catch a diverting chalkboard strategy lecture but instead got back-to-back commercials for 1-900 numbers. A beautiful and vacuous young bimbo writhed around on a velvet couch, dipping her cleavage and cooing into the camera lens.

"Hi! My name is Tiffany, and I need someone to talk to-oo. Would you like to tell me your innermost secrets? I'm so-oo interested. Phone now! I'm waiting for your call."

Lonely men will pay three bucks a minute to hear such mewings.

I used my tongue to squeeze some air through the base of my bridge, making a "tsk" noise (a source of fun I didn't have when I was young), and did some mental arithmetic. Not too long ago, a man could have had the full-bodied attention of a girl called Cherry, room included, for less than the cost of fifteen minutes of a breathy female voice on the phone.

During my own formative years, back in the fifties, self-abuse was still considered man's greatest shame, the furtive resort of pizza-faced adolescents forced to risk blindness and hairy palms in this ignoble practice until they could earn the favors of a real live sexual partner.

But then (hah!) followed the liberal sixties, when onanism came into great repute as the agnostic and enlightened middle class taught their children that beating off was the most progressive thing anyone could do with an idle hand.

Now its popularity has risen to the point where young men don't even bother to court young women anymore. Due to their fear of sexually transmitted diseases and the high cost of a restaurant meal, the upwardly mobile have dropped out of the mating game altogether, preferring to go home alone, order a pizza, and put a call through to Tiffany.

I've been harboring the view that the ancient taboo against masturbation was instituted, and should have been upheld, for the perpetuation of the species.

I sprawled gracelessly in Julian's recliner and enjoyed the new commercial for diet Pepsi, which has a lot more taste than the current product. Ray Charles sings, "You got the right one, baby," and the three pretty girls "Ooh-oohing" behind him look just like the original Supreme of the sixties: Diana, Mary, and Flo.

I've read three different versions of the Supremes' story so far, and with each one, I hoped it would end differently, that this time Flo would pull it out and emerge as a star solo act. But history keeps turning out the same.

I flopped down on the floor and stretched my limbs while the earnest Robert Krulwich tried to get into my punkin head the policy differences between our economy and Japan's.

After his segment, the next commercial began, "What is a loving parent to do?"

This rhetorical question was put to the viewing audience by a distinguished-looking actor in a sincere gray suit.

"Your child no longer communicates with you. He is failing in school. You don't know who his friends are." The actor registered his great concern for the camera lens. "If your child is on drugs, you are not alone. Call us for help at the most experienced drug treatment program in the region. We care."

Then the "We Care" logo was flashed on the screen over the name of a local private hospital whose heartfelt concern embraces only upper-income dopers. The detox program being advertised costs five thousand bucks just to get in.

I heard soft slippered footsteps in the hallway, and my better half wandered in to join me, wearing a red brocade robe I'd given him for Christmas.

"Anything new with the war?"

"At this time of night?"

"It's morning in Kuwait." Julian eased into his recliner. "See? This is coming over live."

CBS's military analyst stood at a map of Kuwait explaining invasion strategy while drawing squiggles that looked like a football game plan.

I moved up to a hassock.

"Why do you men like war so much?"

"Sometimes it's necessary."

"Oh yeah? What possible good is this one doing? I mean, besides giving Bob Hope a new lease on life."

"We had to save our allies in Kuwait. Didn't we?"

"You mean the billionaire sheiks."

"We couldn't let that peaceful little country be brutally invaded, the people massacred."

"Last month, the Soviets brutally invaded Lithuania and massacred people, and we didn't get involved then."

"Because the Soviets are our *friends* now."

"They weren't our friends when they invaded Afghanistan, but we sat that one out, too."

Julian reached over and patted my shoulder as though explaining something to a slow child.

"There's no oil in Afghanistan, dear. You think we're going to fight over yak butter?"

"We have oil of our own, right here in Louisiana."

"It isn't only money at stake. Think about it, Margo." He raised both arms up to the heavens, Hitler-style. "Desert Storm is good for the morale of the whole country! Let's numb people's fears about the recession with the opiate of patriotism." He brought his arms down again, making wavy tracks in the air. "Look how a whole industry has grown up around this war thing."

I caught his drift. "More posters, more T-shirts, more war toys. Hell, there's even some guy named Goldstein up in New York making a fortune selling Saddam Hussein dartboards."

"You see? And CNN has quintupled its ad rates."

"Not to mention that Grumman is doing a booming business in F-14 fighter planes."

"And sales on flags are higher than they've ever been."

"You're right, Neg. That's certainly more important than human lives."

"The effect is far more profound than the mere economic." He stretched his legs out and crossed his ankles in velvet slippers. "After the savings and loans debacle, which we know will cost us five hundred billion dollars, we could all use the distraction. This vicarious adventure takes our minds off rising taxes and plunging values."

"Yeah, and think about all we're learning from this."

"Right. We're learning scads."

"I can now prattle with some authority about governments and leaders of countries I couldn't even find on a map three months ago."

"Exactly."

Then there are the tips on weapons deployment given by every network's pet retired general, and a new lexicon has thundered into common usage. I've been learning that SCUDs are Hussein's evil missiles and Patriots are our good missiles that blow up SCUDs, and a flier's "ordnance" means his load of bombs.

What's more, a "Wolf Blitzer" isn't a weapons system but a reporter with a beard.

Nine

February 15, 1991

Dr. Myra Birnbaum took off her glasses and gestured with them.

"There's not much creativity involved in a forensic sculpture. It's mathematical."

"She's being modest," Frank interposed. "Myra has real talent."

The sculptress accepted the compliment with a shrug. "Of course, it's the bone structure that determines the shape of the face to begin with. All I had to do was make a plaster cast of the skull, then add 'flesh.'" She patted a mound of pink clay. "We have a table of measurements to indicate how much clay to add to each feature, naturally taking race and sex into account."

Then she turned to indicate an iron pedestal, draped with a dish towel. "You'll pardon my flare for the dramatic. Are you ready for the unveiling?"

"Sure," I said. "What could be worse than the bare skull?"

Dr. Birnbaum removed the towel carefully, not to drag it over the surface. "Of course, this isn't his real hair. But this wig is a close match. I made the eyes blue. What do you think?"

Frank gave a soft, low whistle. "You're a great artist, Myra. He looks real." Then he walked around the exhibit and studied it from all angles before allowing, "But I don't know him. How about you, Margo?—Margo?" Then he noticed that I was just standing there gaping. "You recognize him?"

My heart was thumping so hard I had to cross my fists over it.

"Eric Dowd!"

Frank's sigh of relief came out like air escaping from a balloon. "You knew him then?"

"Yes . . . I . . . " The artificial face resembled a waxwork. But now that it was a person and not just a Halloween skeleton, I couldn't look anymore. I turned my back.

"I knew him."

"Fine. So?"

"Eric was this . . . this young hippie who used to hang out with the showgirls. Really nice . . . nice kid." I addressed a muscle chart on the far wall. "He . . . he acted like it was a privilege just to do things for us, you know?"

"Take your time," Frank said. "It's all right."

"Eric would, like, run errands for Sheila. He carried crates of drinks for Reggie . . . walked me to the bus stop after work. . . . Sometimes he'd spell Jimmy at the door when he took a break. We all liked him."

Frank must have taken his pad out. "Where was he from?"

"Somewhere up north is all I remember. The kid didn't talk about himself much. Once I asked him how come he wasn't in the service, and he sort of stammered and couldn't answer. You know? So I figured . . . maybe he was a draft dodger."

"Myra?" Frank was scribbling. "Can you give me some pictures?"

"They're all ready for you, Chief."

I heard, but didn't see, a shuffle of photos, and Frank said, "He looks even more human in these."

"He's supposed to," Myra said.

* * *

Diamond Lil's was the only club on the street that still had an all-girl show and was proud enough to advertise the distinction on a flyspecked poster out front.

GIRLS! GIRLS! GIRLS! FEATURING HOT RED SHEILA CASEY!

And there was a three-foot poster of said attraction in the last stages of her costume, photographed in black and white and painted over with watercolors. I believed the poster hadn't been changed or needed to be changed since the early seventies.

I nodded to the doorman and entered the dimly lit club, where "Mood Indigo" was wailing from an old jukebox. A few doughfaced tourists sat over drinks and gave rare attention to the show. The feature act, Sheila Casey herself, was up on the narrow stage now, still in orange spangles, still doing her old routine, hanging on to the curtain as she gyrated exactly as I remembered. Even her hair, teased into a bouffant, was as long and as red as twenty-one years ago. It was swinging and natural then, limp and dyed now. But through the haze of cigarette smoke and under the pink lights, she seemed not to have aged at all.

For the finale of her act, she peeled off her bra and G-string just as always and finished with the same double split, earning some uncharacteristic applause from the bar leaners.

The manager, slumped on the last stool, was someone I didn't know. He looked me over without moving his chin off his hand.

"Here about a job?"

"No. Could I go back and talk to Sheila?"

He didn't care where I went or whom I talked to, so I passed on through to the dressing room, exactly like every other dressing room: a long mirror, a row of chairs, four tired strippers.

Sheila was still dressed as she had left the stage, in G-string and pasties. She turned to me and smiled. "Hi, Cherry," as though we'd been working together only the week before.

So even in graying middle age, I was still Cherry to her, brought into her fantasy of time having stopped for both of us.

"Hi, Sheila. You danced great tonight."

"Thanks." She pulled a heap of orange spangles off a chair and patted the seat. "Sit down. Where you dancing now?"

She had turned back to the mirror and was teasing her hair to make the pouf even bigger.

"I've . . . um . . . quit show business. Now I'm writing a column for the newspaper."

"Oh yeah? That's groovy—I don't get a chance to read much."

I nursed a hope. If today were still yesterday for her, then a twenty-one-year memory might be fresh and clear.

"I'm working on an important story. Will you look at a photograph for me?" and I handed it over, faceup.

"Sure—oh my God, it's *Eric!*" She clutched the picture in both hands. "Ooh, my honey! Where did you get this?"

I couldn't tell her how the photo had been manufactured.

"The police gave it to me. I . . ."

"But where is he? Where's Eric?"

"I'm sorry. He . . . died."

"Died? You mean . . . When?"

"Twenty-one years ago."

Tears filled her eyes then and spilled over and down her cheeks. "Oh, I *knew* it, Cherry! I guess I always knew it."

Then in the flash of that moment I remembered the handsome blond boy who sat in the center of the bar, gazing up adoringly at the titian-haired girl onstage, and she dancing just for him.

And I remembered even how *I* would smile at them and say, "You two are *so* in love."

But there have been so many loves in and loves out since that year of our youth that I don't smile about it anymore. Or believe in it.

"You were seeing Eric, weren't you?"

"Every night. My honey was very attentive and genteel." A clean bar towel hung on the mirror, and Sheila used it now to wipe her face. "He always took me out to dinner. Usually at White Castle, but sometimes we'd go and splurge at Fun's."

"Weren't you? . . . " I stammered. Cripe, I'd never be a money interviewer. "Weren't you intimate?"

"Oh, yes." She sobbed. "The first time he held me, I just melted into his arms. I couldn't help it." Her voice was muffled in the towel. "We were too much in love to wait."

"How long did you go out with him?"

"Exactly seven weeks and five days."

"I'd say you have a phenomenal memory."

"I was keeping track." The towel was damp now. "When my period was late for the first time in my life I knew I was pregnant."

"Pregnant?"

"I remember the day I told him, too. It was June twenty-first."

So Eric Dowd was still alive on June 21.

"How did he take the news?"

"Like it was the best day of his life. He jumped up and down and clapped, you know?" Sheila's eyes were still wet, but they shone at the memory. "And he laughed and shook his adorable curls in that cute way he had. And then my honey said if it's a girl we'll name her Raquel, and if it's a boy we'll name him Keith, and we'll hurry up and go for our blood tests so we could get married before I started to show. Like I said, he was very genteel."

"So he planned a wedding."

"As soon as we could." She wrung the towel in her square hands. "But he told me he had to go clear something first."

"Clear something?"

"So it'd be legal. Anyway, that's what he said when he walked me home. But he promised to come by the next night and we'd look for an apartment."

"Then did he come by?"

"No." Sheila's voice dropped. "I waited right there at Madame Julie's for him like we agreed. I even stood out by the door when I wasn't dancing onstage and kept looking up and down the street because I'd know his cute blond curls even three blocks away." She tilted her head at me. "But he didn't come. Something must have happened."

I realized she must have told this story to herself countless times, maybe hoping, in one of the tellings, to find an answer to the mystery of two decades.

"But you still expected him to show up."

"Of course I did. He *promised*. So the next night, I stood by the door and waited again. And then the night after that. And I kept on dancing and standing and looking up and down the street for those blond curls." She squeezed her hands together. "I never got off my feet."

Did I remember her hopeless vigil? I had some vague recollection of a showgirl in a flowered wrap who stood under the marquee hour upon hour, making anxious small talk with the doorman while her eyes never stopped moving through the crowds of reveling tourists.

"So the other girls laughed at me and said, So what else is new? The dude just used me and took off like I was trash, the way men always do girls like us. Wise up, they told me." Distractedly, she untwisted a pastie, and her nipple beneath it was brown and shriveled. "But I knew my honey loved me. A girl has to understand when someone loves her."

"She should," I said quietly. "I'm sorry to have to tell you this. Someone murdered Eric, maybe the very night he promised to marry you. His remains were found at Madame Julie's."

"I knew something must've happened to my honey. But I thought maybe he was arrested for pot, or he got amnesia or something like that." Her false lashes were coming unglued. "Whatever it was, I was sure he would come back to me as soon as he could."

"Is that why you never left Bourbon Street?"

"I couldn't. Because then when my honey got well and came back, he wouldn't be able to find me, don't you see?" She looked at me intently, and her eyes were still beautiful, red and blue. "I had to be here for him. So I just stayed and danced. And every night I would dance as specially as I could and look out in the audience for him. I figured I'd know him no matter how old he got or bald or fat, and I tried to stay exactly the same so he'd know me. Don't you understand that?"

"No. I would have stopped waiting."

"But all the time I've been here dancing and waiting for him to come, my honey was right there and he *couldn't* come. He *did* love me, Cherry. That proves it."

"I'm sure he did. Were you really pregnant?"

"Really. Yeah. After another month, the other showgirls said I couldn't have a kid for a guy who ditched me, and they all chipped in for a hundred and fifty bucks for Doc Knight."

"So you had an abortion."

"No." She turned in her chair and flipped open her purse to take out a photograph. "Look here." Its resemblance to the one I'd shown her was eerie. A living version of the death mask.

"Eric's son?"

"Keith. He's a Marine lance corporal now, and he's just been shipped out to Saudi. Wouldn't his daddy be proud of him?"

"Very." If only he knew. "Do you remember Eric spending time with anyone besides you?"

"He went on two or three trips with Kathy."

"Where did they go?"

"Her room, I guess."

"Oh, you mean 'trips' like LSD."

"I was never into drugs, but Kathy always had access, so Eric would give her the bread to score some golden sunshine, and they'd go somewhere and drop."

"I didn't remember the kid was a head."

"He told me he was trying to get inside himself, but then he used to spend the whole afternoon just staring up at ceiling tiles, so he figured he'd try TM instead."

"Where did he get the money for the acid?"

"I don't know."

"He didn't have a job?"

"Not unless he panhandled while I was at work."

TEN

I met Frank in the unofficial police headquarters, Darnold's Doughnut Shop. He was sitting in front of the cruller tray and didn't look around as I slipped onto the stool next to him.

He met my eyes in the mirror. "Did you learn anything useful?"

"I can tell you that Eric didn't disappear voluntarily."

"No one gets plastered into a wall voluntarily, Margo. Have a doughnut?"

"Yes, I'll take one of these jelly numbers." Expertly, I turned it over to start eating at the jelly injection site so it wouldn't squirt out at me.

"*I've* learned something useful." Frank moved his mustache to one side. "No thanks to you."

I swallowed a bite and said, "I'm holding my breath."

"Madame Julie's was mob-connected."

I let my breath go. "Oh, that."

"Yes, *that*. And you knew all the time, didn't you?"

"I knew half the joints on the street were mobbed up one way or another."

"Which way in this case?"

"The usual way." Frank should have understood the game, and I resented the interruption of my doughnut. "When Les Freiberg took over the club, his own stake was no more than five thousand. Burt Amusement furnished the stock, jukeboxes, and everything else. Freiberg ran the place and gave fifty percent of his take to the nice man who came around on Monday nights. Everybody was happy."

"So the syndicate was a silent partner in Madame Julie's. And you never made a connection between them and a body integrated into the construction?"

"Eric wasn't part of organized crime."

"Maybe he tried to deal himself in."

"A naive young hippie?"

"But he wasn't." Then Frank grinned the grin of all-knowing.

"We ran a name check on your Eric Dowd, and we found a man of that name and description who just happened to disappear twenty-one years ago. From Pittsburgh, Pennsylvania."

"Now we're rocking! What do we know about him?"

"Quite a lot. They faxed us his yellow sheet."

"Eric had a record?"

"Long as Highway 90." Frank put a photocopy on the counter between us. "He called himself a construction worker, but actually Dowd was a career criminal."

"I don't believe it."

"He started when he was ten with truancy, then went on to shoplifting, burglary, grand theft auto. . . . By the time your man was eighteen, he'd graduated to ripping off drug dealers. The last entry on his sheet had him wanted for killing an undercover police officer in March of 1970."

"That doesn't sound like the Eric I knew. He was so nice and helpful."

"The guy would have been on his best behavior, don't you think?" Frank tapped the paper. "They made an intense search for Dowd throughout the tristate area, but he never turned up. So they figure he let his hair and beard grow and disappeared into the hippie underground."

"He did an Abbie Hoffman?"

"What better camouflage? One hairy, unwashed flower child looked much like another."

"Now that you bring it up, I remember that districts like Old Town in Chicago and Hashbury in Frisco were teeming with draft dodgers."

"All hiding from the law with the heartfelt support of their contemporaries." Frank made a face. "So Dowd only had to present himself as a different kind of fugitive."

"I get it. Hippies accepted civil dissidents, but armed robbers weren't in fashion."

"Exactly."

I ate my delicious, fresh doughnut in unbecomingly large pieces before saying, "I've got something to add, Frank. I found out that Eric was in love with Sheila Casey."

His mustache twitched skeptically. "Do tell."

"He made her pregnant."

"There's proof of love all right."

"Not in itself, but Sheila says that when she told him he was about to be a father, Eric was thrilled with the idea and wanted to get married right away."

"That's her version. But I have to look at this from all angles, you understand?" Frank stirred his coffee, which had got so cold, the fake powdery stuff wouldn't dissolve. "What if Dowd's reaction didn't quite go by the script? Suppose when the girl bore him the happy tidings, he didn't react with wide-eyed gratitude for impending fatherhood. Suppose this punk did what most punks do, laughed at her and said it was *her* problem."

"I'll admit that would be more in character with the Eric on the police blotter."

"So suppose poor Sheila went into an hysterical rage." He orated like a prosecutor addressing a jury. "Then she picked up a handy wrecking tool and caved in her faithless lover's skull."

"Then you're supposing that she dragged him to the wall all by herself, propped him up inside? . . . "

"It's possible. You said the girl was a champion gymnast. She must have had muscles."

"But, Frank, if she hated Dowd enough to kill him, why the dickens did she bear and raise his child?"

"Guilt."

"There's something else that puzzled me." I wiped my hands on a napkin. "Sheila mentioned that Dowd was scoring acid, so he had an unexplained source of income."

"It was well explained. He was a crook."

"If so, what kind of crook? Dowd wasn't selling dope. According to Sheila, he was just buying and using it. I combed the newspapers for two months and didn't find any unusual reports of robberies, so rule that out. If he'd been a burglar, where would he have stored and fenced the loot?"

"Now you've got my interest." Frank gave up on trying to dissolve the white stuff and put his spoon down. "You tell *me*."

"I have no idea. But I'd bet if we discover how Dowd was getting his money, that will lead us to his killer."

Eleven

February 16, 1991

I was dreaming that I was in a dirty dance with macho Patrick Swayze. I had just tripped over his knee when the phone jarred me awake. Without any clear thought, I picked it up and growled hello.

"Hello, is this Mrs. Fortier?"

"Ahmm?" was my cynical, noncommittal answer, which is supposed to discourage salesmen but never does.

"Good morning. My name is Andy Norgaard. I'm the editor in chief of *Southern Lavender* magazine."

"Really?" I loosened up. "I never miss an issue."

"I'm so glad, because I would like to do a profile on you."

"Me? But why? *Southern Lavender* is for the gay community, and I'm straight."

"We know that, Mrs. Fortier. But we also know that you're sympathetic to our concerns. For one thing, we appreciate your column about the Domestic Partners Act."

That's when I should have asked, "For what *other* thing?" But instead, I just said, "Sure, I'll meet you. I value my gay readers."

When I rolled out of bed, Julian was sitting at the dining room table. It took me a moment to remember it was Presidents' Day, so he didn't have to go to his job at the import company.

He looked from his paper to me to his watch. "Why up so early? It's only one-thirty in the afternoon."

"Ugh." I lurched on through to the kitchen for a Coke.

"Would you like some French toast?"

"Nah," I popped the top and inhaled some caffeine. "My stomach won't be awake for hours."

"I can't eat, either. I keep thinking about that poor fool in Massachusetts."

I carried my Coke back to the table. "I'm tired of feeling sorry for Dukakis."

"Not him. I refer to the poor man who just doused himself with gasoline and set himself on fire to protest Desert Storm. That's the most extreme peace demonstration I ever heard of."

"That's horrible, but not original." I took another medicinal swig. "He might have been imitating the Buddhist monks who immolated themselves in Saigon back in the early sixties."

"You mean the Vietnamese had their own peaceniks?"

"It wasn't about peace." I'm only four years older than Julian, but I'll grab any chance to display my slightly longer memory of events. "The monks committed ritual suicide to protest the Diem regime and their persecution of Buddhists. Madame Nhu used to sneer at the martyrs and refer to them as Buddhist Bonfires."

"Madame who?"

"Nhu."

"Who knew?"

"She was President Diem's sister-in-law. Madame Nhu came to the U.S. to drum up support for the despots in Saigon. She was chic and beautiful, so she got all the media attention. They called her the Dragon Lady."

"I was only a kid at the time, but now I remember. So it was a beautiful woman who pulled us into that filthy debacle?"

"She convinced enough big shots that Saigon was the only bastion of democracy in Indochina, but all her wiles couldn't save the Diems. Madame Nhu was safe in the U.S. in 1963 when her husband and brother-in-law got their final comeuppance from their own army."

"But some countless U.S. soldiers and innocent Vietnamese were forced to share in the comeuppance." He grit his teeth. "And it was all too vicious and senseless for any claim to glory."

"That's true, Neg."

"The generation that followed us still has to learn that."

A couple of seasons back, CBS had a series about Nam called "Tour of Duty." It was well written and acted. But every time the platoon captured a hill at the cost of lives, or lost a man to a sniper, it just reminded me of what a total waste that war was. The soldiers' bravery and sacrifice were all for nothing.

"The peaceniks of the era were right," I admitted, twenty years late. "Even the draft dodgers, and the traitors who ran off to Canada and Sweden. Even those unwashed, bearded, pot-smoking hippies who went underground and preached irresponsibility and the breakdown of the establishment and barricaded themselves in deans' offices and sat in and lay in and sang, 'We shall not be moved,' were all right about the war."

I'd almost finished the Coke by now. The sugar was metabolizing, and life had almost got to be worth living.

Julian asked, "What happened to Madame Nhu?"

"Last I heard she was living in Paris. Very comfortably, too, with the money she spirited out of Saigon before the fall."

"I'm happy to hear it."

"And now I remember a joke. It went: What uses five gallons of gasoline but doesn't go anywhere? And the answer was: A Buddhist monk."

"That's a nice joke."

I got to my feet and tossed the can into the recycling bin. "I need a touch-up. Andy Norgaard is coming to interview me, and he may want pictures." I stopped in front of the mirror and fluffed my hair. "I hope he wants pictures."

"Who is Andy Norgaard?"

"The editor of *Southern Lavender*."

"What?!" Julian almost never shows emotion, but now he looked as close as he gets to angry. "You should never have agreed to meet with someone like that."

"I'm just going to say a few words for his magazine. I don't want anyone to think I'm a homophobe—I should wash this mirror. Me of all people."

"Andy Norgaard doesn't represent the homosexuals of America. *Southern Lavender* is edited for the lowest denomination of gays." He wrinkled his patrician nose. "It's the fruit equivalent of supermarket tabloids."

"If that were so, Julian, the man wouldn't be coming here. After all, there's nothing sensational about *me*."

"Nothing we would want revealed."

Twelve

February 17, 1991

I dreamed that Jacques d'Amboise was trying to teach me to dance, twirling me around the floor with virile grace. He offered instruction in his macho, streetwise accent and manfully pulled me upright every time I tripped over my own big, awkward feet.

Finally I blurted, "Oh, Jacques, this is *hopeless*. Why don't we just stop right here and tear off a piece?"

Then Jacques held me at arm's length and looked incredulous.

"In front of the whole sophomore class?"

I looked around us and, sure enough, there we were in the center of a high school gym in Harlem. And from the bleachers, four hundred pairs of chocolate eyes gawked at the exhibition.

"Oh, fuck!"

Then the school bell rang— No, it was my phone.

Morning and chilling reality.

I rolled out of bed and picked up the receiver expecting Frank with some marvelous new clue. Instead I got the adenoidal drone of Caroline Landau, one of those petrified Garden District matrons.

"Hii-ii, Margo! Guess what?!"

"Thrill me."

"The Vice President himself will be in town the fifteenth of next month, and the Republicans are giving him a dinner. You've simply *got* to come."

"Sorry, Caroline, but I'll be doing something else that night."

"What?"

"Staying home."

"You would rather stay home than meet the vice president?"

"No contest."

Being a hard-news reporter means never having to endure those long-winded, butt-numbing, fund-raising banquets again. I flopped back on my pillow, a contented *ex*–society columnist.

But I had congratulated myself too soon. The next sound to emit from the answering machine was the unwelcome voice of Felix Dune. With the worst will in the world, I picked it up as Marty Allen.

"Hello dere."

"Yeah. Right. You got any news for me, Margo?"

"Sure. Here's an item of interest. Stevie Wonder just walked into a fish market, pulled out a hundred-dollar bill, and asked for a half-and-half party."

"No, he didn't. Listen, by now you were supposed to have more on that twenty-one-year-old dead hippie case."

"There are just a few details about the murder I haven't worked out yet."

"Like what?"

"Like who did it, how, and why."

Then came the sound of his drawing in smoke and blowing it out. "I'll enjoy that joke later at my leisure. Millie's screaming to get back to features, so you'll have to take the column again."

"No, I can't! Not yet!"

"After all, that's what we hired you for, Mrs. Julian Fortier."

"Well, actually I'd love to but . . . uh . . . I haven't been to any charity balls this week. What would I write about?"

"Never mind the charity balls. You want to prove you're a real reporter? Okay, I've got a good hard-news story for your column. Charlie Roemer's jumping parties."

"You mean he's finally *admitting* he's a Republican. That's no story."

"Call it what you want. But since the governor will be running for reelection on the GOP ticket, that leaves the Democratic nomination up for grabs."

"And victory to the grabbiest."

"So, here's our story. State Senator Dickson's people just called to say he's announcing for the slot. Your mission is to interview him and try to make it sound interesting."

"Cripe, let me save gas. I can write the interview without talking to the guy at all." I stood up and caught sight of my slatternly self in the dresser mirror. Bad move. I used my hairbrush without looking. "Dickson will climb up on his soapbox and holler: 'We got t' have respect for our *police*. We got to build more prisons and string up drug dealers. Make the death penalty *mandatory* for every offense greater then shoplifting! . . . ' "

Felix chortled at his end. "That'll be about it, but you still have to get it directly from him."

Then I gave him an item about a Polish crooner who was trying to get bookings as a Fabian impersonator which I actually made up.

The front lawn of Senator Dickson's Georgian house was stuck all over with election signs. Here was a yard-scaped illustration of how a man keeps power in Louisiana.

He must chart his course early in life, get very political, try to pick winners, put his money down, holler at rallies, be counted at caucuses, buy beer for the faithful electorate, and steadily increase his circle of influence until he has assembled an extensive symbiotic network of favor givers and receivers.

I trod the flagstones up to the porch and tried the brass door knocker, which barely showed over a blue-and-white campaign poster blaring, DICKSON'S THE ONE.

(Well, that line has worked before.)

"Mrs. Fortier?"

The young man who answered looked like a Ken doll, with blond hair, a perfect nose, and eyes in cornflower blue.

"Ooh . . . yes. That's me. Mrs. . . . uh . . ."

"I'm Ron Dickson." The doll stayed cool, no doubt accustomed to stupefying women like me with his gorgeousness. "My father has been looking forward to your interview." He smiled and made dimples.

"Oh, yeah . . . uh . . . " I put out my hand, and he clasped it warmly. For one ridiculous second I wondered if Ron Dickson liked older women. But I don't do that stuff anymore, so I just pulled myself together and nodded graciously as a Fortier matron should.

"Thank you, Ron. Are you going to join us?"

"Oh, no. I have a meeting with the Young Democrats—but I *would* like to talk to you again. I *love* your column."

"Thank you. *I* love . . . " But before I could think of something acceptable to admit loving, handsome Ron Dickson had waved and sprinted out the door, leaving me alone with my fantasies.

I smoothed a blur of lipstick in the hallway mirror and tried to smile whimsically like Diane Sawyer.

Now that I'm too old to be loved for my beauty, at least I can still be loved for my column. God is good.

Senator Dickson met me at his office door. "Evenin', little lady." He affected the "Southern Politician" look with light blue linen suit and ribbon bow tie. "Sure was obligin' of Felix to send out his prettiest reporter."

"If you want to flatter me, you just go right ahead." I took the chair he indicated, which was as soft as a cradle. I had to sit on the hard edge to keep from flopping over backward. "Your son Ron is very charming."

"Yeah, best one I got, from my second wife." Senator Dickson enthroned himself in his desk chair, which put his head about a foot higher than mine. "Ron's going to follow me into the family business."

"Politics?"

"We call it servin' the people of the state o' Looziana."

I pulled out my tape recorder and put it on the desk between us. "If you want to say anything off the record, just push this button here."

"Yes, ma'am."

I unfolded my list of prepared questions and pitched my voice low to sound like Linda Ellerbee.

"Senator, you are being mentioned as a leading candidate for governor."

"Raht. My friends have been askin' me to run."

(Every candidate ever born went into politics only because his friends *begged* him to. It was nobody's own idea.)

I imitated Catherine Crier for the next one, unclicking my pen and gazing at him shrewdly. "You are known as a conservative legislator. But now that Roemer is turning Republican, what are your chances of outflanking him on the right?"

"None, so I'm not goin' to try. And I have a flash for you, Miz Fortier. It's the *liberals* who are goin' to sweep me into the governor's office." Then he sat back in his swivel chair to regard the effect of that pronouncement.

For a moment, I forgot who I was trying to be and just sputtered. "Senator . . . uh . . . you have always been a hard-liner. Why would any liberals vote for you?"

"Because . . . " Now he stretched out and crossed his legs like a lazy country lawyer. "Because *I'm* the only candidate who supports legalization of drugs."

"Wha-at?!!" I dropped my pen in my lap, picked it up, and dropped it again. "*Which* drugs?"

"All of 'em. Cocaine, crack, you name it."

"But why?"

"To cut down on crime." He waved his arm as though presenting a circus act. "You see, the only reason addicts go out robbin' and stealin' is the highly inflated price o' drugs. If they could just get all they want for the actual price of manufacture, they'd all stay in their own neighborhoods and get high. They wouldn't have to bother decent people."

"What about the effect on the user's health?"

Dickson sat up and fixed me with his best courtroom gaze.

"Tobacco kills three hundred thousand people a year. You want to outlaw that?"

"I would if I could. How about the damage done by people driving under the influence of drugs?"

He parried quickly, practicing his debate rhetoric on me.

"No worse than the toll racked up by drunk drivers. You want to bring back prohibition?"

"It wouldn't work. Tobacco and alcohol have been grandfathered in. But there's still a chance to stop drugs."

"You're dreaming, Miz Fortier. There's no chance at all to stop drugs." He stabbed the air with one finger. "But we can stop the crimes *caused* by drugs if we make them accessible."

"Senator." I leaned over the recorder. "I could make a long list of famous actors and musicians who died because of drugs. Not because they couldn't get them but because they got all they wanted and that was too much."

"So they were self-destructive fools. They chose their own paths."

"You can argue that, but what about the babies?"

"Whose babies?"

"The *addicts'* babies who are born addicted themselves. Then there are the babies who are abused and neglected because their *parents* use drugs."

"*Those* babies?"

At that, Senator Dickson reached across his desk and punched the Off switch on my tape machine. It stopped whirring.

"Miz Fortier, you want me to be honest with you?"

"That's what I was hoping all along."

"Let's be practical about this, little lady." He lowered his voice as though the walls had ears. "People like you and me aren't going to go on drugs. It's only the scum of society that use 'em. And we don't need their kind, anyway."

"You mean the inner-city kind."

"That's the idea." He smiled for just him and me. "If those welfare blacks want to wipe themselves off the face of the earth with drugs, *I* say *let* 'em."

"You're proposing a sort of voluntary genocide by lethal injection."

He rapped the desk smartly with the flat of his hand.

"Ha! *Now* you've got it!"

Thirteen

An old Cajun stoop sitter smiled and waved as I loped by and I smiled and waved back.

"Evenin', Mr. Guidry."

Three times a week I go jogging, or more accurately hopping along, huffing and puffing. It feels bad and looks worse, but this awkward display keeps my complexion clear and my figure down to a manageable size twelve. I still try to take care of my looks just in case I may need them again someday.

"Evenin', Miss Ida."

My usual route leads from our house in Bywater all the way down to Faubourg Marigny, the neighborhood just this side of the French Quarter. Marigny is an arty little community with a storefront playhouse, an open-mike café, and a gay bookstore. In my column I refer to Marigny as Greenwich Village South. The local cops just call it Homo Heights.

It was almost five-thirty, according to the cheap plastic watch I wear out jogging; time to turn back home.

As I puffed along North Rampart Street, it seemed that every house had a big flag out front or a huge yellow ribbon tied in a bow with a little flag sticking out of it. Or a picture of a flag on a sign saying, WE SUPPORT OUR TROOPS. I stopped and read the small print under the caps: "We at Popeye's Take Pride in Supporting the Men and Women of Desert Shield. . . ."

Considering that the soldiers have spent six months subsisting on sand-coated MRE rations (which they call "Meals Rejected by Ethiopians"), Popeye's would do better to airlift some of their fried chicken instead of putting out patriotic signs.

In the late sixties, there was a vignette on PBS featuring James Earl Jones as an ex-con. The setting was the inside of a Trailways bus, where the stoic Jones was pressed into conversation by some fellow passengers, young students. Begrudgingly, he revealed that he had written to a certain lady the news that he was being released from prison and would be riding this bus through the town where she lived. Should the lady want him back she was to so indicate by tying a yellow ribbon to the big tree near the bus stop. If Jones didn't see it there, he would just stay on the bus and ride through.

After that came the suspense as the students all craned their necks eagerly, hoping to catch sight of the signal.

Then in the final scene, the bus pulled up in front of the tree, which was shown to be *ablaze* with yellow ribbons. Every branch and every twig had a crisp yellow ribbon tied up into a festive bow. Then Jones, wordlessly, pulled his battered suitcase down from the luggage rack and got off the bus.

In 1972, the studio group called Dawn (which later performed as Tony Orlando and Dawn) hit the charts with a musical version of the story, then after that everyone recorded "Tie a Yellow Ribbon" but me.

In 1979, the Ayatollah's gang of hoods took an embassy full of Americans hostage in Tehran and held them for 444 days. Relatives of the hostages displayed yellow ribbons from their trees and porches with the vow that they wouldn't come down till their loved ones were returned.

Last August, when Bush launched Desert Shield, relatives

of troops deployed to Saudi Arabia also began displaying yellow ribbons outside their homes and on their persons. Now the movement has snowballed to the point where the ribbons are tied around every beam, mailbox, and telephone pole and you're almost considered a traitor if you don't have one of them dangling somewhere.

Sometimes on Thursday nights, when I'm watching James Earl Jones on "Gabriel's Fire," I wonder if he remembers starting this whole yellow ribbon thing.

I jogged past the vacant building on the corner of Montegut, where the couple still crouched in their doorway, the young man and woman huddled together, wrapped in their thin blanket. I acted as though I didn't see them, and they acted as though they didn't see me.

Back in the sixties, living was easy. If a hippie didn't have a place to stay, he could always crash with a friend, sleep in someone's van, or roll out his sleeping bag in Audubon Park. In the daytime, he could pick up some eating money panhandling. "Spare change?"

It wasn't a question of poverty or hardship then. We all considered this just a cool phase of "Outta bread, man."

I passed a side street where a pink frame house seemed to have an unusual number of visitors for this time of day. I looked up to locate the welcome sign and, sure enough, there it was overhead: a pair of running shoes, tied together by the laces and flung over the power line. A wordless advertisement that crack was sold here.

I gave the place wide berth and jogged along 2800 block, where I counted three very old cars with very new bumper stickers proclaiming, I'M PROUD TO BE AN AMERICAN!

Now I glimpsed a man about two blocks away and walking toward me. Drawing closer, I could see that it was a black man and looked him over, ready to jump into the street before he came within reach or to circle the block if I had to. But when I got within twenty feet, I saw that it was just a working man in his forties, wearing a mechanic's shirt, limp and grimy from a day in the grease pit. I stayed on the sidewalk and nodded politely as I jogged past.

Muggers in the city: I've learned how to pick them out and then to avoid them.

Usually it's nearly dark by the time I hit my last mile, and honest men are hurrying home, tired and rumpled. But the young criminal is fresh and smart, as his day has just started. He walks slow because he's not strolling: he's hunting. He wears no hat because that would blow off when he has to run away. His shirt and trousers are freshly ironed and loose fitting. Underneath he'll be wearing a colored T-shirt and tennis shorts so he can shuck the outer layer in seconds and change his appearance. He wears athletic shoes for silent walking and fast running.

Often two muggers will work and prey together but split up to seem less menacing. I can spot them though, because they are the same type and dressed similarly. One will walk half a block behind the other, but at the same pace, a slow, stalking pace. Or they will take opposite sides of the street, again at the same pace. Then when the unsuspecting pedestrian strolls into their territory, they'll converge on him or her in a pincer movement.

A female victim is simply thrown to the pavement and her purse jerked from her hand. For a man, a knife or maybe a gun will be shown.

"Give it up! Give it up!"

The man hands over his wallet, too scared then to be angry, but, of course, the anger will erupt later. Then he'll be angry with himself for not fighting back like a TV hero, angry with his wife for sending him to the store after dark, angry especially at the city.

"I'm getting out of this %#@*! place! I'm moving us somewhere it's safe!"

Maybe not this time, but someday he's likely to become part of the fleeing middle class. He may move so far out into the country that he can leave his front door unlocked all day. To some burg so small that only the *jail* has barred windows and doors.

Out-of-towners ask us why we remain in New Orleans, living behind iron grates, supporting an alarm system fit for a bank, and paying ten percent sales tax for the privilege. Julian just says he's the sixth generation of New Orleans Fortiers, and that seems to explain it for him. My standard answer is that I'm too lazy and too decadent to live anywhere else.

I don't attempt a speech extolling our cultural advantages because I hardly ever attend gallery openings or the opera. I don't stress the city's quaint ambience, either. When I ride through the French Quarter these days, I never stop to study the ironwork balconies or watch the street performers or listen to the mellow horns wailing through the doorways of jazz clubs. Nor have I chatted up any Jackson Square artists in some twenty years.

Maybe I found my way here because the mystique suits my self-image. "Margo Fortier of New Orleans" sounds better than "Margo Fortier of . . . " anywhere else at all. And this place has a hum of business and real life happening that I want to be part of. I want always to sense the dynamic of the city. I want to look out my window and see streets and houses and people, not trees. Even bad people are better to see than trees.

There is an old Yiddish tale about a traveler who kneels by a pond and out of curiosity addresses one of the fish.

"Tell me, friend, what is it like, living there in the water?"

"Oh, it's awful," the fish avers. "There isn't enough food for me here, the bigger fish try to eat me, fishermen try to catch me, and sometimes it gets so cold that I can't even move!"

"Why, that all sounds terrible," the traveler says sympathetically. "So why don't you *leave* the water?"

The answer is that the fish *can't* leave, and neither can I.

* * *

When I finally dragged my aerobicized body through our front door, Julian had solidified in the living room, concentrating on the TV. "Come in and watch this," he called to me. "It's really a good one."

I stood behind his chair and watched the TV over his head. After a minute, I said, "We saw it before."

"No, we didn't."

"I clearly remember, Neg. Daffy Duck marries some rich duck for her money, and she makes him clean her house all day while her spoiled little duckling gives him hell."

"No, you're confusing it with the one where Sylvester the cat married a woman for her money, and her spoiled little fat kid gives him hell. We saw that a few weeks ago."

"You mean they used the same story?"

"There are no new plots, Margo."

"Cripe, a remake of Looney Tunes." I sat on the floor to stretch. "Hey, you know what? They were there again. Those people in the doorway."

"What doorway?"

"The doorway of that vacant warehouse on Montegut. I see this young couple, a *white* couple, just sitting there, wrapped in a blanket, day after day, even when it rains. What the deuce are they doing there?"

"Living there, I guess. What's the mystery?"

"But why live in a doorway? What's their motivation?"

"I don't suppose it's their habitat of first preference, do you?"

"They seem able and healthy. Between them surely they could make enough money to get a room."

"Maybe they're not what they seem. Why don't you ask them?"

I bent forward and grabbed my toes.

"How could I do that?"

"In your own tactful fashion." Julian screwed up his face and did a bad imitation of my nasal Yankee accent. " 'Excuse me? Why do you two choose to live here in this doorway rather than, say, a condo with a pool uptown, or maybe a mansion out by the lake?' "

"Because I can't ask them anything without forming a relationship." I held on to my toes for a count of ten. "Those people are bound to prey on my sympathies and involve me in their problems. They might even expect me to give them a place to stay."

"That's some kind of Oriental notion. If you save a life, you become responsible for that life."

"Hey, I bet I know why they're living in the doorway." I dropped the toes. "They're students of Eastern philosophy trying to find themselves through denial of material things, the way Gandhi did."

"Yes!" Julian snapped his fingers. "That *must* be it. A joint thesis on the transcending of the spirit. Did you happen to notice a typewriter there in the doorway with them?"

"No, but they might have had a notebook under the blanket."

"I'm sure you're right."

I grabbed his chair for support and got to my feet.

"Listen to this, Neg. Margo Fortier, girl reporter, got a real scoop today."

"Do tell. Was Zella Funck caught 'en flagranté'?"

"Even better. This is a bombshell from Senator Dickson. You'll never guess his campaign promise."

"Electric bleachers for mass executions of drug dealers?"

"Quite the contrary. He wants to legalize street drugs."

"Criminey. Who is going to vote for *that?*"

"Twenty years ago, you and I would have, remember? Back then pot was considered a victimless offense upheld as a felony only by the greedy establishment."

"I know. I used to keep up with it in the *Playboy* Forum. The laws against pot were enforced by a conspiracy among the liquor and tobacco lobbies." Julian shook his head. "That bunch at NORML had us convinced marijuana was harmless. Since then we've learned that smoking pot sears the lungs, numbs the brain, and dries up the gonads."

I said, "When I was growing up in the fifties, drugs were considered part of the arcane underworld. A universal taboo. It was *our* generation that made them cool and brought them into the mainstream. Now look at what the hell we started with our liberal ideas."

"It appears that we pried open a veritable Pandora's box and shook the monstrous little imps all over the landscape." Julian heaved a long sigh. "Let's not blame our youthful selves, dear. As a great statesman named Winston Churchill once said, 'Any young man who is a conservative has no heart, and any old man who is a liberal has no brain.'"

Fourteen

I located my old friend, Regina the male barmaid, in my own newspaper under Church News. He was billboarded as tonight's principal attraction in the auditorium at St. Germain's.

There was a good turnout for the lecture, especially considering the topic wasn't something relevant to modern times (like "An Amateur's Guide to War Profiteering" or "How to Go Short on America's Future") but "Letting Jesus into Your Life."

I crept in behind the crowd and took one of the metal folding chairs in the last row.

I decided long ago that religion has been so down-marketed over the decades that it's become the refuge of the old, the poor, the black, the foreign . . . So tonight I was surprised to see how many young people were in the audience: upwardly mobile, college-educated, bran-chewing, nonsmokers at that.

The program began with a troop of full-figured gospel singers in robes leading us in a medley of gospel songs. Then the organ played a sacred-sounding fanfare, and the Reverend Reginald McCann himself strode out onstage and accepted the whooping ovation with raised palms. His eight-hundred-dollar Armani suit was a long reach up from the paisley ruffles I'd remembered on dear old Regina.

The reverend commanded the podium, and the noise ceased as abruptly as though turned off by a switch. Then he joined his resonant baritone with the choir for three verses and a chorus of "Just a Closer Walk with Thee" before beginning his speech.

"I have sinned!" he confessed to us all in stentorian tones. "Oh yes, I'm not going to stand up here in the sight of God and tell you I never sinned! I listened to the Devil in my youth! I drank, I used drugs, I did EEVEEL things. So EEVEEL that I wouldn't even name my sins in the presence of these good Christians sitting here before me. But I found Jesus, and he revealed to me that there's no sin that I, a little man, can *commit* that *He*, a great God, cannot *forgive!*"

I snuck a peek at my watch behind my purse, the way I used to during Mass. But the people around me all continued to stare straight ahead like zombies, caught up in the sermon.

"Some of you are sinners, thieves, murderers, drug users . . . " the good reverend ranted on. "Let our Lord Jesus Christ take you to His bosom and cover you in His *warmth!* God has a *plan* for you! Open your mind and heart to *accept* it. Once you dedicate yourself to serving Him, there will be no more *doubt!* Even through all trials and pain ahead, you will have happiness and strength. Your soul will be *healed!*"

I tuned him out and entertained myself thinking about some good sins I would enjoy committing if only I had the chance. Then I parted with a buck when the collection baskets were passed.

After the sermon, the gospel choir started up again for the finale. The hymns were the ones everyone knew, "Amazing Grace" and "Rock of Ages," almost nonsectarian. I stood up and sang with the rest, and that was public spirited of me because in an audience full of white people, I was one of the few able to support a note.

Bucking the retreating crowd, I showed my press pass and

got ushered back to the room behind the stage. By now the star attraction had removed his sweat-soaked jacket and shirt and sat panting in his Newarkie, fanning himself with a hymnal.

"Good evening, Reverend McCann," I said.

"Good evening, Mrs. Fortier."

Then I bent and hugged him. "Hi, Regina."

He kissed my cheek. "Hi, Cherry."

"You gave some fantastic show out there. I think you could outpreach and outsing Jimmy Swaggart in his prime."

"Maybe." He reached behind him for a chambray shirt. "In terms of the collection at least, it was a very successful sermon. But did any of it sink in?" He shrugged into the shirt and buttoned it without looking. "Will any of those converts out there leave this place determined to become a more worthy person?"

"From their reaction, I'd bet most of them did."

"But will even *one* make a real change in his life? It would all be worth it for one." Reggie pulled on his windbreaker. "Alexander Pope said, 'Make yourself an honest man, and be assured there's one less rascal in the world.' "

"Hey, that's pretty good. So why didn't you quote Pope to those people out there instead of that primitive Bible stuff?"

"Because those people out there didn't want intellect, they wanted comfort. And for that you give them religion, not philosophy." He winked in the mirror. "Horatio."

" 'Gimme that ol' time religion,' " I quoted on my own. "Now, I'll admit that sometimes I feel like eating Pablum because it used to taste really good. But I know I've outgrown Pablum."

"No you haven't. Try it some night when you're all alone, with hot milk and bananas."

"I might just do that." I put a hand on his shoulder. "You have something special, Reggie. I'll bet your parents are proud of you now."

"No, they're both dead." He said it robotically, without

inflection. "And they died without ever being proud of me."

"I'm sorry. For them."

"Me, too. I heard they were all alone at the end. My brother, the straight one, was busy with his family, and no one else had time for Mom and Dad." He looked up to change the mood. "What brings you here, Cherry? In search of God?"

"More like the Devil. There was a murder at Madame Julie's back when we were working there. I hoped you might remember the victim." With that I gave him the photo of the clay sculpture.

"It's Eric! Someone killed him?" He quickly handed it back. "Oh, I just adored that boy. But I can't say I knew him personally."

"No? He hung around the club a lot. And since your apartment was right upstairs, you might have had a few drinks together after hours."

"Never happened. Eric was straight."

"Do you recall his spending time with anyone in particular?"

"I recall that he liked you girls. Sheila Casey in particular."

"I already talked to Sheila. She's devastated."

"She would be, poor thing. Eric spent time with Kathy, too, but . . ." Reggie shrugged. "That won't help you. You ought to go look up Samantha."

"You've seen her around?"

"Mercy! There's no missing *that* girl, still dressed head to toe in purple, day and night. I call her Moby Grape."

At that moment, a cute young red-haired guy poked his freckled face in the door. "Reverend? The TV crew is outside."

"Lovely!" The man of God made a quick check in the mirror. "Tell Angela I'll be right there."

The freckles whisked out again, and I watched the door close.

"Well, well, Reggie. Has that little crumpet 'found Jesus,' too?"

"He's looking real hard."

Fifteen

February 18, 1991

Frank did the driving. Like most men, he always had to be behind the wheel, and in control, even though he didn't know where we were going and I had to point the way.

"You go past Juno Street and turn right at Juniper. Go slow or you could miss it."

"I hope Miss Herd has a good memory."

"She may know more than any of us. Samantha is the only flower child from our youth who has remained a flower child."

The Silver Lamp Book Store had posters in the window alerting us to "Guided Meditations," "Psychic Healing" lectures, and the latest published wisdom of wackos like Shirley MacLaine and Uri Geller. They call the scene New Age now, and chakra stones have replaced love beads as the neckwear of choice. But the hippie era is still alive in places like these and the philosophy is just as spacey.

My opening the door activated a glass wind chime, ping-pinging in five tones. Frank frowned at the noise and looked around the door frame as though for electrical charges before entering. I'd have bet money that no one that big and that black had ever entered the place as a customer.

Dennis was behind the counter, as he had been every night since the shop opened.

"Hi, Virgo," I said. "We've come to see Samantha."

"You want a private reading?" Dennis squinted behind his thick glasses. "She gets thirty-five dollars."

Frank choked. "Thirty-five dollars for what?"

"Samantha's our most popular tarot reader. Her predictions are famous."

Frank folded his arms. "She can keep the future. We're here about the past."

I pointed with my thumb. "He's a cop."

"I know." Dennis drummed his fingers on the appointment book. "She's just beginning a group psychometry demonstration in the big room."

"We'll sit in."

"That will be five dollars each."

Before Frank could object, I hastily paid for both of us, then grabbed his elbow and steered him back to the big room.

Samantha was holding forth from an arm chair surrounded by her audience of believers, who huddled excitedly at rows of folding tables. As we found two vacant chairs, she was already into her explanation.

". . . So every object has its own aura of energy, and everyone has an ability to feel it. Mine is enhanced because I've spent years sensitizing myself to the vibrations."

Samantha still wore her hair as long as in the old days. But now only the ends were dark and the beginnings gray. Her long purple dress was shabby and frayed at the sleeves. I wondered for the zillionth time why people who are renowned as psychics never seem to have any money. If this poor soul can't even find herself some gainful employment, how is she supposed to locate somebody else's elusive karma?

"I'll start the demonstration now." Samantha stood up and wafted over to the nearest table, where all and sundry articles were thrust out at her from trembling hands. She took a gold fountain pen from an agitated fat woman and carried it back to her chair.

"This is a very warm, loving person." She rolled the pen between her fingers.

"It was my mother's," the fat woman said.

"She has passed over, hasn't she?"

"Oh, yes!" the woman said. "I miss her so much!"

"But she's with you now. I sense your mother standing right behind you with her hand on your shoulder. She is telling you she's gone to a beautiful, calm place, and you're not to worry." Samantha closed her eyes. "Something about finances . . ."

"Oh, yes!" the woman blurted. "Mama never thought I had any sense about business."

"Your mother is warning you to seek professional advice. That's what she's saying right now."

"Oh, *yes*, Mama! I *will!*" The fat woman clasped her hands together. "Thank you! Thank you so much!"

Next, a thin, shorthaired woman who looked sexually neutral held out a crystal on a ribbon. "This belonged to someone I loved very much who died recently."

Samantha held the crystal up to her cheek. "She died of something carried by the blood."

"You're right! She was my cat, Mindy." The querent clasped her hands to her breast. "She died of feline leukemia last month."

"Yes, I see her now. Mindy is resting and healing, bathed by a blue light."

"Does she—" The woman choked. "Does she know how much I love her?"

"I feel that she does," Samantha assured. "And she loves you just as much." The seer shut her eyes as though listening to a voice no one else could hear. "Mindy says she'll be coming back to you early next year, as a healthy new kitten. You will know her by her special markings."

"Of *course* I will." The woman took back the crystal, clutching it tightly. "I'll go to see every litter until I find my baby." Tears were spilled down her cheeks. "And I'll bring her back home."

"All she wants is to be with you again."

A skinny little nerd in thick glasses handed over his cigarette lighter. "Can you tell me about what's going on in my life?"

"Not your *present* life."

(Naturally not. He *hadn't* one.)

Samantha closed her eyes. "I see a Roman warrior. No . . . you were a *gladiator!* I see you fighting in the Coliseum."

"M-me-ee? But I never fought in m-my *life*."

"Maybe not in *this* life, but you were the greatest gladiator of the fourth century. I can see the emperor Flavius placing the wreath of laurels on your head."

"Far *out*."

Frank was sitting with his arms folded and his mustache curved in a sneer. I whispered, "Give her something to read."

He growled low. "I will *not*."

"Come *on*." I started groping in his jacket pockets. Then finally, out of a sense of modesty, he slapped my hand away and reached into his pants pocket for his car keys, which I pushed into the seer's open hand.

Samantha felt the key holder and frowned. "No! I don't like this person. . . . I see a tall blond man with a lot of hate. Violence and hate! Be careful of him. He's dangerous!" She hurried to return the keys to Frank, who slipped them back in his pocket without a word.

Samantha's private consultation room was just big enough for a card table and three patio armchairs. I sat in the one next to her, close enough to smell the marijuana in her hair. Frank squeezed himself into the other, and it was a tight fit.

I made my apologies and introductions. "Lieutenant Washington is investigating a murder that occurred in Madame Julie's club during the summer of 1970."

"You're talking about . . . " She paused to do the subtraction. " . . . twenty-one years ago? Oh, I can't tell you much about that period."

"But Samantha, you remember *me*, right? Cherry? I wore the fake leopard dress and a platinum wig."

"Vaguely."

I showed her the photo of the sculpture. "His name was Eric Dowd."

"Eric?" Instead of looking, she put her hand on it. "A pure spirit, I can tell. A very good person. But I can't remember relating to anyone back then."

Frank nodded. "On drugs the whole time?"

"No, I just wasn't there at all. You see, I'm a walk-in. In fact, I'm the fourth soul who's inhabited this body since 1970."

That confession rendered Frank incapable of speech, so I picked up the ball. "Eric used to come backstage. Maybe you tripped with him a few times."

"There were a lot of acid trips . . . " She closed her eyes and sang, "Sunshine came softly through my window today . . . "

A Donovan song. Where *is* Donovan now? I touched her arm.

"Samantha?"

She stopped singing but kept her eyes closed.

I asked, "Have you seen anyone from Madame Julie's lately?"

"Anyone? Just Laura."

I hurtled by the mention of Laura, hoping Frank hadn't caught it. "Have you seen Ray Lowery?"

"Lowery? I think I've blocked him. He was evil to the dancers, especially to this Samantha person." She indicated her own body with a vague hand motion. "Too flaked out to count her money. The soul who was in possession then . . . well, she was very unhappy. She only stayed a year."

"I never noticed that."

"I couldn't blame her, either. This planet is such a cold, unfriendly place." She hugged herself. "I'm from Zeefirus on the other side of the galaxy. I can't wait to get back there."

Frank didn't say another mumbling word till we were nearly three miles down I-10.

"Margo?" He shifted into fifth. "*What* in our divine Lord's name is a *walk-in?*"

"Just a change of soul, as the theory goes."

"A change of *what?*"

"Let's say a soul has an important job to do on earth. But he doesn't want to be reincarnated as a baby and waste twenty years growing up."

Frank sighed heavily. "All right. Consider it said."

"So he gets himself reincarnated into a living adult body."

"And how, pray tell, is he supposed to manage that?"

"Some person on earth gets fed up with life and wants out of it. But he doesn't want to commit suicide, see? So he sends a message into the continuum asking another soul to take over his body and brain. Then he 'walks out,' and the new soul with the mission 'walks in.' That's the theory."

"Well, I don't like to put down other people's theories, but I know for a fact that one is absolute nonsense."

"How do you know?"

"Because if it were possible to walk out of a body, I'd have bloody well walked out on *this* one before now."

"Maybe you couldn't find a buyer. Look, Frank, it doesn't matter whether you or I believe in walk-ins. Samantha believes it. So I'd conclude she's less than useless as a source of information."

"The poor woman may have a ventilated brain from pot and LSD. On the other hand, she may know exactly who hit Dowd and is just hiding behind this spacey act. But . . . "

"But what?"

"I'm curious, Margo. How did she do that thing with touching the objects? It must have been a trick."

"Of course it was a trick. Samantha thinks she's a psychic, but she's mainly in the business of telling people what they want to hear."

"How does she know what they want to hear?"

"After years of practice, she's developed a combination of reading people's faces, guesswork, and logic. Then if she can't figure out what the hell to say, she'll tell the client about some glorious 'past life' as an Indian princess or a soldier in Caesar's army. Who can disprove it?"

"But that fat woman with the pen, how did Samantha know so much about her mother?"

"The woman herself told her. She looked so desperate and unhappy that any pro could tell she was in mourning. Then Samantha just said 'Finances' and the fat woman filled in the rest. Who doesn't think about finances in one aspect or other?"

"How did she know about the feline leukemia?"

"She didn't. She didn't even know the deceased was a cat."

"But she said it died of something carried by the blood."

"Almost anything you can die of is carried by the blood, Frank. Cancer, germs, virus . . . you name it."

"So it's all a clever scam."

"Sure it is. Ninety-eight percent of this New Age stuff is utter bull dung. By the way, that key chain of yours . . ."

"Yes?"

"Samantha carried on like it was giving her these really bad vibes. Who had it before you?"

"I have no idea. It was made in the prison shop at Parchman State Penitentiary."

Sixteen

There had been six showgirls at Madame Julie's in June of '71, but Frank wouldn't be told of the last, Laura Pennyson Grant. Pennyson is a New Orleans name nearly as old as Fortier.

Laura was the freshest and prettiest girl on the street that first summer after her debut, flashing the glossy hair, clear complexion, and straight teeth that mark a child of privilege. But Laura Pennyson was totally unaffected for all that, seeming to love everyone and enthralled with every part of street life, a world she was seeing for the first time. She did her act as Pepper Mint, giggling over the name and wiggling her firm equestrienne's behind like a flirty majorette.

That was then.

Today, the Grants' Garden District house is one of the few mansions that has survived as a single-family home. I knocked the ring in the brass lion's nose, and Laura herself opened the door to me. She was wearing the "Ivana" look this season, with high-piled hair and puffy lips.

"Margo! I'm so glad you came by."

She never called me Cherry after that summer we danced together. It was as Mrs. Julian Fortier that I ran into her at a fund-raiser for the Landmark Society in '82. Laura didn't, or pretended she didn't, recognize me from our early days at Madame Julie's, so I always played it that way, too. Until today.

"Honestly, I'm just all beside myself with this benefit for the zoo." She nudged me into the living room. "Do you know I spent half the morning blowing up balloons?"

"We all do what we can."

Her five-carat diamond solitaire refracted the ceiling light as she waved at the colorful pile of balloons against the wall. "Would you like to join me in a drink?"

"If you have something soft . . ."

"Oh, sure." She slouched over to the wet bar, served me a glass of Coke with a napkin under it, and poured herself a vodka martini from a sweating shaker. "I'm always grateful for the paper's support, but I hope you'll give us better coverage than last year. I ran my legs off rounding up celebrities to give the door prizes." She sounded breathless with the exertion. "The weatherman from 'Live at Five' has promised to come."

"That's a coup, all right." I followed her to the couch, and we both sat primly on the edge of it.

"Scoot in the Morning might drop by. I'm crossing my fingers."

After that feral summer, Laura had gone back to Sophie Newcomb College and resumed her life as a proper daughter of New Orleans society, inevitably marrying into another old family and, more inevitably, stiffening into a typical mainline matron, calcified in her self-absorption. Every sentence would begin with "I" or end with "me."

"I'm not here to talk about the benefit." I set my glass on the coffee table atop its mandatory napkin. "We have to discuss something that happened on Bourbon Street twenty years ago."

"What? No!" Laura flicked her hands as though shaking water off them. "Bourbon Street is all in the past. I really can't deal with that now."

"I understand," I said like someone who understands. "That's why I want to keep it just between the two of us. Can you help me do that?"

Hearing it put that way, she resigned with a nod, then half-finished her drink before going on.

"I was heavy into sociology that summer. I've always been a humanitarian." She pointed to the pile of balloons for corroboration. "So I wanted to go across town and hang out with some *real* people, you know?"

"I get it. You just came to Bourbon Street in the spirit of an anthropologist."

"Maybe I did."

"And went native."

She blinked both eyes slowly.

I took out the forensic photo and put it on the table. "I need anything you can tell me about him."

She folded her arms and regarded the picture without touching it. "That's . . . Eric. The boy who used to run down to Felix's for seafood. Right? Yes, he was cute."

"Did you know him well? Ever date him?"

"Maybe once. Eric and I went to see *Myra Breckinridge* at the Orpheum. I dated a lot that summer."

"In the spirit of sociological research."

"I tried every experience. Humph. I even let Jimmy the doorman take me to Pontchartrain Beach." She rolled her eyes. "But he turned out to be all hands on the Ragin' Cajun ride. And worse than that, he bleached his hair. He thought he looked like Mike Love."

"But he didn't."

"No." Her voice wavered like a radio with weak reception. "Not that I was out for any heavy involvement anyway. Nineteen seventy was just my summer of wild oats."

Most of Laura's "wild oats" had been dark in color, as I remembered. A selection of jazz musicians she would meet at the Society Page after the strip clubs had closed for the night.

But I didn't interrupt with that observation as she faded back in.

"Then Eric got totally involved with Sheila. And she was just as crazy about him. They were such a cute little lower middle class couple, I was sure they'd get married."

"They didn't."

I took a long look around at Laura's antiques. Not bought but inherited through four or five generations.

"Did your parents know about your season of slumming?"

"God, no! They were in Europe that summer." She clasped her hands so hard that they turned red at the fingertips. "If Daddy and Mum had ever even *suspected*, they'd have made a suicide pact."

"Then too there might have been a problem making a good match for you."

"Geoffrey wouldn't have understood about the sociology." She rubbed a spot off her glass. "He majored in economics."

"I'm sure."

Geoffrey Grant learned enough about economics to buy his way to power in the Republican party. He'd got himself elected to the State Central Committee and now reigns as the permanent Power behind many temporary thrones.

"Tell me, Laura. Have you seen anyone from the street lately?"

"Heavens no!" Then she caught herself. "Well, I've seen Samantha. But only professionally."

"You mean as a psychic?"

"What else?"

I had to pull my jaw back up manually. Why would a woman who has everything seek advice from one who does business in a plywood cubicle?

"I don't want to get personal but . . ." Yes, I did. "But what would she be able to advise you about?"

"Business matters," she said with a perfectly straight face. "Last year, Geoffrey wanted to approach Donald Trump about a joint real estate venture. But Samantha warned us against buying real estate with anyone who's going through a divorce."

"Afflicted fourth house," I said, really to myself.

"I think she used that term. So anyway, a few months later, Trump filed for bankruptcy. You see, she really is psychic."

"Psychic my foot; that's kindergarten astrology. Home, family, and real estate are all connected."

We were interrupted then by the sound of the front door banging open, and tall, broad Geoffrey Grant rolled in like he'd just been pried loose from Mount Rushmore. "Laura, call that goddamn gardener back. Those hedges need tri . . ." Then he spotted me and said, "Oh."

"Oh, Geoffrey, dear." Laura scurried to his side, fussing and twittering.

"You know Margo Fortier. The columnist?"

"Yes, Julian's wife." But he didn't smile or make any gesture of greeting. In Geoffrey Grant's bracket, one doesn't have to be nice to people.

"I'm interviewing some friends for a nostalgia column," I sprang up. "Do you remember anything about New Orleans during the summer of 1970?"

Laura looked panicky and held her breath. Her husband just regarded me like a Jehovah's Witness flapping Bible tracts.

"I can't help you. I was on guard duty up in Alexandria."

"I was very proud of him then," Laura gushed. "He served his country honorably."

"I got out of the draft," Grant said curtly, and headed for the stairs. "I'm taking a shower."

"Your favorite towel is all ready," Laura called to his retreating back. "I'll be right up." Then she looked helpless, which was an accurate look. "I have to go hang up his clothes. Geoffrey's a very exacting man."

"Charming, though." I drew a card from my purse and put it on the table. "That's my home phone number. If you remember anything more about Eric, it will stay between us." I moved to the door.

"Cherry . . . ," she whispered. " . . . I mean Margo."

I turned back around, but she didn't meet my eyes because this was a confession.

"When I was working down there with you girls, I used to . . . well . . . feel like a real person. That doesn't happen anymore."

"I know."

Seventeen

It was only seven-thirty, so the night shift hadn't yet begun at the Cabaret Paree. The day barmaid perched on the beer box, yawning and checking her watch, waiting for cash-out time.

"Goin' to the dressing room," I said on my way through, and went unchallenged.

Out in the rear courtyard, I knocked at the door of paint-flecked wood planks, but there was no answer. I turned the ancient brass knob and stuck my head in. "Excuse me?"

The only occupant was a naked transvestite with a long blond wig and silicone implants. She was concentrating on her manicure so beckoned with an elbow. "Bring it on in, hon. You coming to work here?"

"Not tonight." I shut the door behind me. "But I was in the lineup twenty-one years ago. I'm returning to the scene of my youthful glory."

"If this was glory, you must have had a deprived childhood, dearie. My name's Misty."

"The place was a lot different, though," I told Misty. "We had carpeting when I was here." Now the floor was bare cement like the courtyard outside. "And there were more lightbulbs then."

But we had all been young, pretty girls forever primping at the mirror. Any night could bring a Prince Charming into the club, or a talent scout, or a fashion photographer. We would apply our false lashes with surgical adhesive, gaze at our reflections, and imagine that we were stars in the ascendant.

Over these two decades, the cast had changed, and bright lights are the enemy of drag queens with their artful illusions.

"Management doesn't furnish us any amenities." Misty wiggled her glistening nails. "Between shows, we have to run out front and hustle drinks."

"Where's the glamour?"

"Nowhere."

There was no surface clean enough to sit on, so I just stood in the middle of the dingy room and tried to picture the way it had been in June of 1970.

Samantha always sat on the first stool at the mirror, where she would burn colored candles as sorcery: green for money, blue for love, red for vengeance. The red one was kept lit like a votive light in front of a rag effigy of Ray Lowery.

Sheila would be on the second stool, teasing her red hair, and Toby of the swiveling tassels would sit next to her, speaking softly, sometimes reaching over to touch her hand.

Kathy, the pill head, used to arrange her stash in rows according to color and variety. "I've got to go on now." She would snatch up her baton. "Nobody touch my dope."

"Nobody wants your fucking dope," I would say, sitting cross-legged on the rug in the corner. I would be rereading a letter from my warrant officer in Long Binh or composing a blatantly carnal reply on lined loose-leaf paper.

Laura (a.k.a. Pepper Mint) never stayed in the dressing room between shows. As soon as she finished her act, she would pull jeans and T-shirt over G-string and pasties and run the streets. But every hour she managed, though just barely, to be out onstage again when her music started playing.

"Say . . ." Misty broke into my reverie. "Were you working here around the time someone walled up that poor hippie?"

"Yes. Were you?"

"Oh, not *me*, honey. *I* was only nine years old back then."

"Bitch."

Eighteen

Frank stood up all of his six feet, two inches and looked down at me sternly, then turned his back and stared out the window at the prison across the alley. When he finally spoke his piece he sounded weary. "You've been holding back, Margo."

I conveyed wide-eyed innocence. "How's that?"

"You went to see Laura Pennyson Grant this afternoon."

I sidled into the wooden chair across from his desk.

"So, that's my job." I hoisted my nose insouciantly. "I'm a society columnist and she's society."

"She was also Pepper Mint for one heady season. When my man showed me her photo, I remembered the sixth girl in the lineup." He paced around the bare linoleum, felt his pockets, then shook his hands in disgust. "I don't smoke anymore. My wife says, 'You want to live a long time; don't you?' I say, 'What for?' Hell."

"Frank, I'm *shocked!* You had me followed! After all these years, you don't trust me."

"I think I could have trusted a stripper named Cherry, but not the well-married Mrs. Fortier." His already dark eyes darkened further. "Obviously, protecting your position with your uptown peers takes precedence over a murder investigation. Back to you."

"Be reasonable. Laura couldn't have had anything to do with the murder. So why smear her name?"

"Your friend had a pretty strong motive. What if Eric found out she came from one of the fine old families and threatened to publicize her summer in the sun?"

"He wouldn't have done any such thing."

"The side he showed you."

"Laura wasn't physically able to carry a grown man out to the courtyard, prop him up inside a dry wall, and hammer two cedar panels over him."

"Not alone. No. Incidentally, where was her husband that summer?"

"Doing a Quayle up at Fort Polk."

"In Alexandria? Now, that's a whole two hours away."

Nineteen

February 19, 1991

The Soviets have decided to play referee in the Gulf War crisis, and they certainly mean well. The Commies have come up with this cockamamie Eight-Point Peace Plan that would require the Iraqis to withdraw from Kuwait within thirty days.

Well, my gosh, what *wouldn't* they have time to steal within a whole entire thirty days.

(Everything they haven't stolen *so* far.)

The Soviet plan looks pretty good to Saddam Hussein, and he has publicly conceded to four out of the eight provisions. But President Bush responded to the Soviet peace proposal with a plan of his own. Specifically, he orders the Iraqis to start getting their asses out of Kuwait not within the Russkies' thirty days but by noon tomorrow. (Read his lips.) As usual, Bush purposely rhymed "Saddam" with "Adam" knowing that pronunciation makes the name mean "despised shoe cleaner" in Arabic.

Jim Turner, Esq., plied his trade in a prewar bank building on Carondolet Street. The place was so old that the elevator was still operated manually by a septagenarian who closed the steel grate door, then pulled a brass lever to get us moving. He stopped at every floor, actually a little above or a little below, never quite flush with the floor. The Law Offices of James Turner occupied the south wing of the fourteenth.

At the front desk, a gray-haired man with a torso like Lou Ferrigno's sat in a wheelchair pounding the hell out of a word processor. His nameplate said JACK GILLEY, PARALEGAL.

I stood in polite silence till he finally sensed my presence and looked up from his smoking machine.

"Excuse me, Mr. Gilley. I'm Margo Fortier."

"The columnist?" He grinned widely. "Well, I'll *be*. Jim *told* me he met you. Right now he's out at lunch with the state chairman, but I expect him back by two." He put a hand up as though signaling a waiter. "Erin? Mrs. Fortier's here."

A delectable ingenue with auburn hair detached herself from a row of desks and clip-clopped out to the reception area. "Would you like something to drink, Mrs. Fortier? Coffee? Wine?"

I took a chair and settled for a Coke while marveling that Turner kept a beautiful girl hidden away in the back and a middle-aged handicapped guy out front.

"Tell me, Jack . . ." I declined the proffered glass of ice cubes and sipped my Coke from the bottle. "How do you like working for Mr. Turner?"

"I like it fine. The boss pretty much leaves us alone to do our job."

Actually, he probably left the paralegals to do *his* job.

"Really?" I fluttered my lashes. "He must trust you with a lot of responsibility."

"He ought to." Gilley had taken a cup of coffee for himself, black and too hot to drink. "We both fought in the First Division over in Nam. The Bloody First they called it."

"I've heard about the Big Red One. They say y'all had the highest casualty rate."

"Bet on it. See, I bought this chair stepping on a mine in Quon Loa. Now, I didn't want to live on any pension; I'm a *working* man. So the Veterans Administration put me through vo-rehab and I studied to be a paralegal." Gilley slapped the arm of his wheelchair, which wasn't a motorized one. He'd come by those muscles honestly. "Then after I got qualified, I spent months putting in applications all over town. But you know what? Not one single lawyer even contacted me for an interview. Seems they like to have a cute girl sitting at the front desk, not a crippled-up vet."

"I'm sorry." I really was. "That bites it."

"But finally, thank God, I heard from Jim Turner. He remembered me."

"Remembered you from Vietnam?"

"Yeah. Turned out Jim and I served together in Lai Kie during my first tour."

"What kind of soldier was he?"

"Sharp, that's what he was. A by-the-book man, just like he is now. And he volunteered for every bad mission that came up. Killed a lot of the enemy."

"Sounds like a real hero," I said with no detectable sarcasm.

"You better believe he was. We all thought Jim would be an important man when he got back to the world, and sure enough he made it big. And he took his friends right along with him." Gilley looked around his office with some satisfaction. "You know, when he took me on, he already had two paralegals. He didn't even need me."

"Maybe he did."

I heard the door open behind me, and Gilley snapped smartly to attention. I spun around to greet the hero of Lai Kie.

"Hi there, Margo!" Turner bombasted. "Glad you got back to me."

"Hello, Jim." I rose and clutched my purse tightly in both hands to discourage him from trying to shake one.

"Come right on into my parlor." He grinned and held open the door of his private office. I preceded him inside, then wandered around the room instead of taking a seat. I presumed he wouldn't mind my distraction because he had turned the place into a one-man hall of fame for himself featuring every kind of souvenir of his war years.

I touched the sharpened point of a bamboo pole.

"This is a punji stick, right?"

"How did you know?"

"I had a warrant officer over there. He said the dinks liked to dig a hole, line it with these spears, and cover it with camouflage."

Turner nodded twice. "Then the GI falls in, and we find what's left of him impaled on the punji sticks. It's not easy to pull him loose, either."

"What a thing to save."

"If we forget the past, we're doomed to repeat it, right?"

"Not with the same cast and scenery. There won't be any punji sticks over in Saudi."

"SCUDs and poison gas. Same difference."

I moved on to the next exhibit. "You kept your Colt 45?"

"Who didn't?"

I took the automatic off its display stand and rubbed the polished walnut stock. There was a clip in place. "You keep it loaded?"

"I'd better. We keep a lot of cash in this office."

"Why? Who pays you in cash?" He just looked at me as though waiting for the next question, so I moved on to the most telling souvenirs of his tour, medals framed behind glass.

Turner's Combat Infantry Badge was on top, shaped like a long rifle. And beneath it his Vietnam Service Medal, yellow, red, and green with a dragon, rested between the National Defense Service Medal and the Army Medal of Honor.

"I see you have a purple heart," I said.

It was a gorgeous gold-rimmed cameo of George Washington. (I'd have worn it as a pendant.)

"Took a bullet for that."

"Two Bronze Service Stars."

"I volunteered a lot."

"And a Good Conduct Medal."

He chortled. "That was the hardest one to earn."

I finished my museum tour and sat down. "You've made yourself quite a reputation."

James Turner's desk looked like it had never been used except to hold his feet, which it was doing now.

"Yeah. My friends tell me I should run for office, statewide. If Senator Dickson weren't in the race, I'd take a shot at old Charlie Roemer."

"I just interviewed Dickson. He's definitely in the race."

"I've got more name recognition than he has down south. After all, I'm known for fighting for the poor."

"But only against the rich."

"How's that?"

"They say you never sue unless there's a lot of money to be made."

"Hey, I've got to run this office, you know?"

"Right. I have some news about the hippie in the wall. He's got a name now."

Turner's voice was tight. "What name?"

"Eric Dowd, from up north. You remember him?"

"Yes." He swiveled his chair around to face the array of war medals. "Dowd used to hang out in the club all night till closing. He was a nice kid from what I could see."

"Did he tell you he was a draft dodger?"

Turner's back was to me, so I couldn't see his expression. But the stiffening of his shoulders said much.

"He didn't tell me; but it was around."

"So how does a patriot like you, who was wounded fighting for his country, feel about a man just the same age who ran away from his obligations? Who stayed home and smoked pot while you were getting your ass shot off?"

"Those are bones older than poor Eric's."

"They were new in 1970. You were a decorated soldier.

Wouldn't there be a natural animosity toward a peacenik like Eric Dowd?"

Turner swiveled back to face me. "Hawk kills dove, huh? Are you implying that I would commit homicide just because I disagreed with a man's politics? Where's the profit in *that?*"

"You forget that our generation wasn't about profit. Passions ran strong in those days. The peaceniks were willing to go to jail for their beliefs."

"You sound like you were one of them."

"No, I wasn't into the peace movement."

That was a middle-class preoccupation.

Jane Fonda went to Hanoi, and John and Yoko gave a press conference from their bed and sang, "All we are saying is give peace a chance." I was too busy working for my living to get involved.

What was that war supposed to be about? Oh yes, we were trying to stop the "Red Menace."

That was back when Jesus was still God and he was on the side of the liberals. Us liberals.

So now Jane Fonda has left one of the Chicago Eight for the love of a media tycoon to the ideological right of Vlad the Impaler. And John Lennon's been shot dead, dead, dead.

I scanned the titles on Jim's book shelf: *Gardens of Stone, The Deer Hunter, Ho Chi Minh Trail.*

"You still do some reading about the war years."

"It's something I'll never get away from. At least twice a year we vets get together and try to talk out our feelings."

"Yeah, well, I don't want to probe painful memories, but I'm trying to get a feel of the era. How about telling me what happened after you got out."

"Sure." He sighed. "I was discharged that spring. I'd blown most of my pay on Saigon tea, so I needed some kind of job till classes started at UNO. I was lucky to get on working the door at Madame Julie's."

"And there was no bad blood between you and Eric Dowd?"

"Hell no. Dowd and I often walked home together. We stayed in the same hotel up on fourteen hundred block Canal."

"Which hotel?"

"I remember it was some fleabag over Duffy's bar. Rooms were fifteen bucks a week." He scratched his head. "It's not there anymore. Anyhow, I got along fine with the guy. We used to have long talks about my tour in Nam. Dowd was a good listener."

"It would suit my purpose better if *you* were the good listener."

Turner shrugged. "The guy wasn't interested in talking about himself."

"What did you think when he disappeared?"

"At first I figured he just took off to Biloxi for the weekend. But he didn't come back on Monday. After a while I found out Sheila Casey was pregnant with his kid, so I thought I had the answer. Eric just couldn't handle the responsibility."

"So then he disappeared, leaving all his belongings behind. Wouldn't his landlady have reported him as a missing person?"

"What could he have had in the way of belongings? A pair of hip huggers and a water pipe? Why should she care? He was just another hippie who ran out on his rent."

T<u>WENTY</u>

The penthouse suite at One Shell Square was a set from a Lorimar prime-time soap and the receptionist a little Barbie doll of a girl with glossy platinum hair and pert C-cup bosoms.

"Mrs. Fortier? Yes, Mr. Fortunado is expecting you. Go right in." This was an invitation she seldom was given to bestow so enjoyed delivering it like news of a prize won. She buzzed her intercom and popped up to push open the thick polished door marked Private.

Inside the office, Robert stood at his massive desk and bowed formally. "Mrs. Fortier?" And he held his arm out to usher me to a throne-size armchair done in green leather.

"How gracious of you to make time for me, Mr. Fortunado," I said prissily, and looked down on him from the vantage point of my three-inch heels. He was short, stocky, and balding but reeked with virility, a boar hog of a man in Giorgio Armani pinstripes.

"It's my pleasure."

I took my seat as he closed the door behind us. "There's something I've been meaning to ask you, Mr. Fortunado."

"What's that, Mrs. Fortier?" he asked as the lock clicked.

I crossed my legs to show off the ankle straps and lowered my voice. "Are you still the greatest lay on the delta?"

"Not at all." He walked around me then and perched on the edge of his desk. "Only the greatest *male* lay," and stroked my hair. "How's it goin', Cherry."

"Not bad, Rocco."

His fingers moved from my hair down to the collar of my mink jacket. "This must be warmer than that rhinestone G-string you were wearin' the first time I saw you."

"I'd say so. And this office looks a lot more impressive than the old one: your hat."

He gazed around at the teak paneling to appreciate the irony along with me.

"Yep. Wasn't even a clean hat. So now what can I do for you, girl?"

"I need your input. Do you remember when you used to collect at Madame Julie's?"

"I did more than that. To see we got a fair count, I had to watch the books, check the drink meters, count the house . . ."

"So you can tell me if you ever saw this man hanging out."

I gave him the picture, and he held it at arm's length for a moment, then shook his head. "Maybe he was around, but I'm damned if I'd remember. With all those bare-assed girls runnin' all over the place, how'd you expect me to look at a *guy?*"

"I've heard that same disclaimer before. This boy was a hippie named Eric Dowd. They found him in the wall out behind Madame Julie's."

Rocco gave the picture one more try before handing it back.

"You insinuatin' it was my people who put him there?"

"Who else is famous for losing former adversaries in construction sites?"

"Adversaries, yeah. But who was this kid to us?"

"Maybe no one. But he was a hippie, so he could have been buying drugs. Maybe even dealing."

"My friends were never into the hippie drugs, Cherry. Pot was too small-time with all those amateurs in the market. Every college kid was growin' the stuff in his window box." He wrinkled his Neapolitan nose. "They could make LSD in their chemistry labs. They could buy their ups and downs with a doctor's prescription. Kef was smuggled across the border in student backpacks. The market couldn't be controlled, so we stayed out of it."

"I guess the real money was in smack."

"Real money *then*. Peanuts compared to cocaine profits out there now." He stood up and walked over to his window, which featured the best view of the city, all the way to the river and the Greater Orleans Bridge. "Cherry, when you and I were comin' up, addiction was an aberration. Now there are more users in one high school than we used to have in the whole parish." He turned around slowly. "Know where you can go today to see fifty addicts in a row?"

"Needle Park?"

"Nah. I mean the baby nursery at Charity. They're *born* on drugs. Today it's right out in the open. The users nod out on church steps, and kids play with needles they find in the street. Ten-year-olds quit school to run dope." He waved at the world outside the window. "It's all gone to hell, girl. We don't have any society left to be outlaws in."

"I'm sorry nonprofessionals have cut into your business."

He held his palms out. "Hey, I'm legit. There are a hundred ways I can make money just by shufflin' paper. Look here." He picked up his *Moody's Index* and flipped through the pages. "Tomorrow I could buy a healthy company that's tradin' below book value. By the next quarter I could sell off the assets, suck out the cash, bankrupt the whole operation, and put a thousand heads of families out of work. Then I could show a loss on my books and get a tax write-off."

"That's immoral but not illegal."

"Real immorality seldom is. But I don't want to be a rich man in a depressed city."

"No?"

"No, Cherry. I want to be a rich man in a *prosperous* city. So now I'm dreamin' and schemin' to generate jobs in Louisiana. We've got to bring big corporations to the area. And for that, we have to offer them a competitive tax base, a trained labor force, and safe housing for their middle management." He spread his palms in an "all gone" gesture. "I don't see any way to make a profit for myself there."

"This is how. You bribe the legislature to commission a study, then get them to pay you a half million in consultation fees." I slid the photo back into my purse. "I'm looking for this man's murderer but figured I'd better touch base with you first."

Rocco nodded gravely. "You don't want to stick your big nose where it doesn't belong. I like that." He leaned forward and took my face in both hands. "Well, baby, far as my people are concerned, you can look for your killer, find him, convict him, and smoke him on 'Geraldo.' "

His speaker box buzzed, and he reached behind him to turn it on without taking his eyes from mine. "Yes, Kirstin?"

"The attorney general is on the line," said the box.

"I'm in the shower." He switched it off and shrugged.

I said, "She's a beautiful girl, that Kirstin."

"Yeah, they're all beautiful. But I can't talk to them. Not about the old days. Not about anything." He grimaced. "You know what that bimbo considers an oldie? Elton John. I swear to my mother."

"What did *we* used to listen to? The Doors, right?"

"Yeah: 'I'm gonna love you till the heaven stops the rain.' We played it our first night."

"All night. You know, Jim Morrison is back in fashion now. There's a new movie about him."

"For true?"

"It seems that everything comes around again."

"Yeah, seems it does." He massaged the back of my neck. "Cherry, you and I could come around again. I'd treat you well."

"No thanks, Rocco." I stood up, shifted my purse, and kissed his cheek. "You wise guys have a way of discarding your mistresses in pieces."

He spoke into my hair. "Only if they're bad."

"But I'm the baddest."

Twenty-one

Today was warm for February, ideal for a long, leisurely jog through Bywater. I had done my six miles and rounded the corner of Burgundy when I spied a young black couple, sitting on their stoop, drinking beer and hugging their boom box. They stuck in a new cassette tape just as I passed by.

The number began, "I'm a motherfucker . . ." and the language deteriorated from there. I increased my hop-along pace and hurried on up the block but not before getting an earload of violent woman-hating invective over a skull-ringing downbeat.

By the time I made it inside, it was already after seven, so I rushed to the TV and punched up to channel 12. Swaying across the screen was a line of healthy, corn-fed young people, the girls in fluffy dresses, the boys in three-piece suits, all bright-faced with Pepsodent smiles.

Julian came wandering in ten minutes later and I waved him over. "Come on, Neg! It's Lawrence Welk."

"You kidding?" He walked around the back of my chair. "When we were young, you wouldn't be caught *dead* watching Lawrence Welk."

"You missed Salli and Sandi's duet. That was some great

harmony. Personally, I think they've always been underrated."

"I remember my *grandparents* used to watch Lawrence Welk back in the *fifties*. And he was old *then*."

Welk had just smiled into the wings at Joe Feeney, the Irish tenor, and turned back to aim the smile at the camera. "And now-a we join-a Bobby Burgess-a and-a Cissy King."

The Blenders barbershop quartet, attired identically in tomato red suits, stood in a gazebo set and harmonized to "Lyda Rose" while dark Bobby and fair Cissy tap-danced across the stage, hand in hand.

I pointed to the screen. "He was a Mouseketeer, you know. The handsomest, most talented one in the bunch, too."

"No doubt." Julian drawled. "I wonder what Bobby Burgess is doing now."

I was annoyed. "He's dancing to 'Lyda Rose' with Cissy King. Can't you see that?"

"But *that* was . . ." He tapped my shoulder. "Margo?"

"Hunh?"

"Listen. Do you remember the old 'Star Trek'?" He'd turned earnest all of a sudden. "I mean the *original* 'Star Trek.'"

I kept my eyes on the TV. "With orange shirts and cardboard sets?"

"Right. Now it looks like 'Captain Video' next to the new version. But I was thinking of one particular episode called 'All Our Yesterdays.' The Enterprise crew visited a planet that was about to be destroyed so they could rescue the inhabitants."

"Rescue the inhabitants . . . ," I echoed, to pretend I was listening.

"But when Kirk and Spock beamed down, all the inhabitants had already disappeared."

"Disappeared . . ."

"It turned out they had all saved their own lives by escaping into the planet's *past*."

Welk was introducing the singing Atwell twins from Texas, and I pulled my chair closer to the screen.

"I don't know what you're driving at."

Once inside the house, as per current custom, I turned on CNN for the latest from the front.

The newscaster, as always, sported a toupee that I felt insulted my intelligence. That network's anchor policy must read: "If you want to sit at *this* here desk, you'll go get yourself a *wig*. It doesn't have to be realistic or even match your actual hair, but just get something furry up there on your head."

"Today in the Gulf, our correspondent has been talking to the troops about a threatened ground war."

One freckled GI was interviewed in the mandatory setting, with a jeep in the foreground and desert in the background. "Hussein has kept me away from my family for six months," he asserted for the video camera. "I want to finish what we came here to do so we can all go home."

His impatience is common to most of the men and women who've been squatting on the border since August, eating field rations and cleaning sand out of the machinery. Everyone the reporter interviews is visibly chomping at the bit to move in and fight his way to glory.

After five and a half weeks of bombing sorties, Hussein's military machinery is presumed to be blasted all to hell, so the coalition infantry is free to stroll into Kuwait without fear of resistance.

Most of the great political and military minds have been predicting a ground war as quoted by the CNN reporter.

" 'You can fly over it, bomb it, spit on it, but you don't *own* it till you're sitting in City Hall.' "

Not till the commercial did I notice my answering machine and that the red light was blinking. I played back the message, just one.

"Margo? Are you there? This is Samantha. I went into the

akashic records and found out Eric Dowd is *alive*. If you want more on it, I'll be doing readings tonight at the Silver Lamp."

It was almost eight o'clock, so I had to turn right around and head out again.

The "akashic records" she was babbling about is an imaginary book of all events, past and future, that some trance mediums claim to access. I didn't have much faith in Samantha's psychic powers, but if she were tapping into her subconscious memory, she might have come up with something useful in spite of herself.

Dennis was again (or still) behind the counter and showed no surprise at my reappearance.

"Samantha has just four minutes to her next reading. She told me to send you right in."

The seer's hands were occupied in shuffling and reshuffling her tarot deck. "Peace, Cherry. You got my message."

"Twenty minutes ago." I took the chair opposite.

She touched the Uranus symbol hanging from her bracelet. "I guess you know Saddam Hussein is using astrology."

"How do you figure that?"

"He invaded Kuwait under the strongest aspects. Pluto was precisely fifteen degrees Scorpio. We're in for a long hostility."

I thought about that. Neptune hit fifteen degrees of Scorpio back in '63. That's when Diem fell, Kennedy fell, Pope John XXIII died, and chiefs of state all over the world lost their positions.

Then Uranus hit fifteen degrees of Scorpio in '78. That year *two* popes died, heads of state in Italy, Afghanistan, and Pakistan were murdered, and many more lost their positions.

Still, I said, "It could have been coincidence."

"I don't think so. Remember how he refused to meet on Bush's deadline of January fifteenth?" She was looking over my head at some star map in her mind. "There was a solar eclipse that day, and any astrologer would have warned him against making decisions."

I said, "I remember that Hitler used astrology."

"Of course he did."

"So Churchill hired astrologers of his own to find out what advice Hitler's astrologers were giving."

Samantha's voice was fading out. "Do you think Bush will do that?"

"I think he'll keep this war going till he's thoroughly established himself as Captain America."

"Earth is such a cold place. Humans aren't evolved at all.

"Can you really tell me something about Eric Dowd?"

"I just put his picture in my third eye . . ." She tapped the middle of her forehead. "And today the answer came to me in a white flash."

"You said he's alive."

"He is. And I saw him at the Westside Shopping Center at three o'clock this afternoon." She leaned over the cards. "Listen, Margo. Eric has just been reincarnated as a baby in Gretna."

"A—uh—*baby?*"

"A Libra, I'm sure, so he'll be five months old now." She pulled a piece of paper out of her sleeve. "I got the license number of his mother's car. Here, you can trace it through your friend on the police force."

"For the love of *Mike*, Samantha! What am I supposed to *do?* Interview the *baby?*"

"He may have some anterior memory." She cut the cards into three stacks. "If you gather some belongings of your suspects and let him touch them . . ."

"Right, I can just see that interview. Frank would love it."

"It's one way to get the truth."

"The *truth?*"

She turned over the first of the three top cards. It was the nine of swords: time of danger or endings. "Uh-oh," she said, and then turned up the second, the queen of cups. "That could be you," she said. "Or it could be me."

I said, "I know."

She hesitated at the last card, just biting her lip and staring. So finally I reached across the table and turned it for her. Number thirteen, the black-hooded skeleton, stared up at us both with eyeless sockets.

It was Le Mort, the death card.

Twenty-two

February 20, 1991

"Jangle-jangle!" rang the phone at the top of its bells. When the Moon hits my Venus, I always hear from a woman. Always. When it hits my Mars, I hear from a man. Where is the Moon today? I paged through the ephemeris of my fuzzy mind. Leo. I rolled over and looked at the clock radio. It was barely noon. No friend would pester me at an hour like this. So I curled into the fetal position and left the rude caller to my answering machine.

First came my own voice, flat on the tape. "You have reached the Fortier line," I shrilled nasally. "Please leave your name and message." Then Frank Washington's.

"Are you there, Margo? I think you'll want to hear this."

I didn't believe him and stayed under the covers.

"Samantha Herd was found dead this morning."

Dead? For that I rolled out of bed and picked up.

"Dead? Frank, I saw her last night in her reading room at the shop."

"Well, she was still there this morning, with a knife in her heart. Did you see anyone else around?"

"No, but Samantha mentioned that she had one more client to see. *I* know, Frank. *That* person must have killed her."

"Oh, I agree absolutely. And I can't wait to put out the APB. 'Wanted for questioning: That Person.' "

"I'm on my way to the Silver Lamp."

As I tooled down the Franklin overpass, the man with the sign was there as usual, holding it at midriff height with both hands. The sign was brown cardboard with a crudely lettered bid: I WILL WORK FOR FOOD.

It's a new panhandling gimmick, of course. Or does this disheveled man really expect motorists to pick him up and take him home?

"Just go on out back and mow my lawn. I'll have your plate of stew ready when you're finished."

What guilt-ridden liberals will do instead is stop by the curb for a moment, roll the window down just far enough to stick out a dollar bill, and say, "Here, go get yourself something to eat."

That cardboard sign probably makes more money than I do.

I turned left on 610 and punched up the all-news station.

There were no new developments, so the network crews were trudging through suburbs to ask families of soldiers how they felt about their GIs and whether they were proud or not. That was non-news.

I poked the tuner on up to Lite 105. It was playing "You're in Love" by Wilson Phillips, a pale second generation of the Beach Boys and Papa John. That was acceptable. But then "You've Lost That Loving Feeling" came on, and I punched it right off again when it turned out to be the scuddy Hall and Oates version. The FCC ought to order every recording of that travesty melted down and declare the Righteous Brothers' the only version legal for broadcast.

Mind you, I'm reasonable. I am willing to listen to Don McLean sing "American Pie" for as long as it takes but will not sit still for his assault on the Roy Orbison classic "In Dreams." Orbison *or* Linda Ronstadt can sing "Blue Bayou."

Anyone at *all* can sing "Cherish," with good charts. Even Milli Vanilli, probably.

At the Silver Lamp, Dennis already had his appointment book turned to the night before.

"Okay, Margo. The caller gave the name Ed Smith and asked for the last reading of the night, said he worked late."

"What did he look like?"

"All I can say is that he was a white man, fairly tall. As I told your friend Lieutenant Washington, he had his collar turned up, his hat pulled down. He hardly spoke."

"Didn't that strike you as unusual?"

"Not at all." Dennis closed the book. "A lot of men don't want to be recognized coming to see a psychic."

"I understand. It's not considered macho."

"He paid for the reading with cash. Then he walked out after forty-five minutes just like any other client."

"But Samantha didn't."

Dennis's eyes darkened behind the thick lenses.

"I don't watch the door every minute. I was in the back unpacking Chinese health chimes. Then when I went around to lock up, the light wasn't showing under the door of her room, so I assumed she'd gone home."

"I guess she had. Back to her planet."

"Yeah."

Twenty-Three

I loaded the electric coffeemaker with Community Dark Roast and started it dripping. I never liked the stuff myself, but this is the only service I perform for Julian that's remotely wifey. Magically, he walked through the front door the exact moment it was ready, and I handed him his mug.

"Thanks, Margo." He nodded over the steam. "I was stuck at my desk till they closed the building, and I'll still be up most of the night working."

"I'll stay out of your way."

"I appreciate it."

Julian and I enjoy the basic element for an ideal marriage: we don't get on each other's nerves.

"When you stayed out so late," I followed him into the dining room, "I figured maybe you had a date."

"A date? In Goldwyn's two words: *im-possible.*"

"Why is that? You're a nice-looking guy."

"I'm stunning. But whom would I dare to date? Half the gays in this city are carrying AIDS, and I don't know which half."

"Just so it's not the half that includes you."

"Not me. I went for the blood test again last month. I've

still got my little paper that says 'HIV negative' clutched tight to my bosom."

I flopped into a Queen Anne chair. "You ain't got no fuckin' bosom."

"Ooh, my dear!" He recoiled dramatically. "What happened to your language?"

"I'm just tired is all." I pulled off my shoes and wiggled my toes.

"Dearie me, Margo. I could change your name to Fortier and give you the air of respectability you craved, entrée to all the drawing rooms in the Garden District." He pulled over the silver tray with his filigreed tea service. "But underneath it all you're still Cherry from Bourbon Street. Scratch that sterling veneer and there peeps through—ah—a *rhine*stone. A chipped one at that."

"It doesn't matter, Neg, since you're the only one who sees my rhinestones."

"And of course I'm inured. Because underneath these ten generations of Fortier breeding and the finest schools to be schooled in both here and abroad, *I* am a man with *no* class." He picked up the silver tongs and, by way of punctuation, dropped a sugar lump into his coffee. "None whatsoever."

When I first got a load of those silver tongs, I thought they were maybe for picking fleas off a dog.

When I walked into Le Boucle Restaurant, Ray Lowery was cleaning up behind the tables in the back. He was still the same skinny weasel face I remembered from Madame Julie's but now in a grayer, more shriveled version.

It was two minutes to closing time. The customers had departed, the cash register was locked, and Ray didn't notice me because he was busy leaning on his push broom and regaling the trash collector with some apocrypha about his favorite politician.

" . . . so David Duke goes ahead and rubs the lamp, but the genie who comes sailing out is *black*, see? So the genie says,

'Okay, I'll give you anything you want, but then I'm gonna give every black person in the United States *twice* as much.' So David Duke says, 'I want a million dollars,' and the genie, he waves his arms and—poof!—there's a million dollars, but then he gives every nigger in America *two* million. You see how it goes? So then David Duke says, 'I want a Ferrari Testarosa.' So—Poof!—the genie gives every nigger in America *two* Ferrari Testarosas. Get it? And then the genie, he finally says, 'Okay, now what's your third wish?' So David Duke, he says, 'Beat me *half* to death.'"

Ray laughed loudly and thumped his broom. "That David Duke is no fool, you know? He'll be gettin' *my* vote."

The trashman was shaking his head. "But he's a *Nazi*."

"Not any*more*."

The trashman hefted the fluted thirty-gallon can up to his shoulder.

"Shee-it! I'm gonna vote for someone who was *never* a Nazi."

He made his exit on that line, leaving me alone in the place with my number-one murder suspect.

Ray turned and saw me, then nodded and got back to work, pushing his broom with long strokes.

I said, "Good evening, Ray," and he looked startled. Moreso when I added, "I would like to talk to you."

I'd seen Ray dozens of times over the years but never acknowledged him. I was Mrs. Julian Fortier and he was the cleanup man, period. I'd been assuming he didn't even connect me with Cherry, but in that I proved wrong.

He stopped sweeping. "Okay, Mrs. Fortier." Then he leered. "Cherry. It's been a long time."

I showed no expression. "I'm working for the newspaper now."

"I know; I read your column. Then I tell people, 'Hey, she used to work for me at Madame Julie's, but I can't convince them."

"Nice of you to try, anyway." I proffered the photo. "Do you remember this boy from the old days?"

"How could I remember any boy? We didn't have boys in the show back then." But he accepted the picture and held it up to the light. "Nope." He handed it back. "That face looks sort of familiar, but I can't put a name to it."

"The name is Eric Dowd, and he used to hang around the club. He sat at the end of the bar, brought in the ice, helped you with the stock . . ."

"Listen, I worked all over this street. I managed clubs for fifteen years, and there were hundreds of punks like that, sniffing around the girls, trying to promote some pussy for themselves."

"Eric was only interested in one girl, Sheila Casey."

"Hey, let me see that again?" Ray took the picture back, and a smirk started small and grew. "Yeah . . . now I remember where I saw this face before. On Sheila Casey's kid."

"You're still in touch with her?"

"I see her around, but she never talks to me. Like with you."

I made no apology for my lack of warmth but handed him my card. "You can call me at this number if you remember anything pertinent."

He gripped the card tight enough to squash the engraving. "Say," he looked sly. "If someone helped you catch who did it, would there be a reward of some kind?"

"The poor soul was a hippie, dead twenty-one years. Who the heck would put up a reward?"

"On 'America's Most Wanted' there's always a reward."

"Well, maybe I could arrange one. Where do you live?"

"In the back." He inclined his head toward the rear of the restaurant. There was no space for living quarters, so he must have been talking about a cot in the supply room. "The boss likes me to be here at night."

Twenty-four

I used my lip pencil to make a fuchsia outline. Luscious. My mouth used to be my most arresting feature.

"You have lips that make a man want to kiss you," declared my b-drinking customers, leaning across the bar.

But nowadays it seems half the women in Christendom have gone and got their lips puffed up with collagen or silicone, so mine aren't special anymore. Same with my green eyes and the advent of color contacts. My distinctive features have been ripped off by all and sundry, and I'm left with having to make it on my personality.

(Worse luck. I have a *horrible* personality.)

I stood back from the mirror and put my hands under my breasts. They felt full and round, just right, so naturally the rest of me had to be too fat. I didn't even want to *think* about my thighs.

Should I make the effort to lose a few pounds? Nah. At my age one has to choose. If I dieted down to a trim, youthful figure, my face would look haggard. Not worth it.

I'd rather look like a plump thirty-five-year-old than a slender forty-five-year-old.

The hallway has a full-length mirror where I stopped for final inspection. My peach cocktail suit was both demure and slimming in a midcalf length. I pretended to be posing for a sexy man and instantly straightened my spine, threw my shoulders back, sucked in my middle. Now I had a discernible bosom and even a waistline.

I decided that anything I've lost to age over the years is more than compensated for by custom-fitted clothes, wrapped nails, and hair by Teri Case, stained and painted into a mosaic work of art.

I called to Julian in the living room.

"I'm prettier now than I was twenty years ago."

He answered with a languid sigh, like a Noel Coward juvenile.

"It is a benevolent God indeed Who weakens our vision even as He sucks dry our youth and ravages our beauty." Julian glanced up from his volume of Stendhal in French. "Into your three-inch heels, yet? Are you in love again?"

"Not yet, but . . ." I tossed my hair and looked insouciant for the mirror. "Robert Fortunado wants me to be his mistress. What do you say to that?"

"I say, you should update your will. And don't forget that clause that goes, '. . . to my beloved husband, Julian, my house and all I possess . . .' "

"You've got the wrong idea."

" . . . And *do* indicate cremation. No one will want to scoop all that mess into a coffin."

"Robert's company is Fortune 500. He's honest and respectable now."

"You obtuse little commoner, money does *not* buy respectability. Not in the first generation, anyway."

"But at least he makes me feel like a woman. It's not my fault that very few men past forty are still virile. What would you do if you were me?"

"Ee-oo. Get a tummy tuck, I think."

"There's nothing wrong with my tummy."

"My dear, don't tell me you got all dressed up just for a date with your hoodlum?"

"No, I wouldn't really risk my reputation by dating Robert. That was just a girlish fancy." I looked woebegone for the mirror. "Today I'm going to a sort-of wedding."

"What do you mean 'sort-of'? Either something's a wedding or it isn't."

The "commitment ceremony" was set in the parlor of the Domestic Aid Center, and as with all events here, there were no men in attendance.

The delicate girl at the portable organ started Lohengrin's "Wedding March," and the two principals in gowns of antique satin shuffled in procession up to the altar, followed by four attendants in lilac.

It looked like a puzzle from the old *Humpty Dumpty* magazine: "What's wrong with this picture?"

Jeepers! Two brides!

I'm a traditionalist when it comes to weddings. I believe, for example, that a white dress with veil is for the young first-time bride only (who is less than seven months' pregnant). In the ideal case, the bride would be a woman and the groom a man.

But two people who love each other should be able to commit themselves to the union and make a life together. That's traditional, too. And it's not the people's fault if God saw fit to make them homosexual.

San Francisco just passed an ordinance allowing "nontraditional" couples to register officially as "domestic partners," and I overstepped the purview of my column to applaud the proposition.

"Gay partners should have the same rights as spouses regarding inheritance, taxes, and insurance," I stated for the record. Then I gave the logical reasons for my position in an inciteful essay enhanced with those light touches of wit that are mine alone.

My editor collected two cartons of hate mail over that one.

Same-sex marriages aren't recognized under the law in New Orleans or anywhere else that I know of, but there's nothing to stop people from inviting their friends over and declaring their intentions.

Luella Jenkins, a gay civil court judge, officiated the ceremony wearing her black robe and reading from a leather-bound book.

"Do you, Lorna, pledge yourself to Meg to love and cherish . . ."

This all seemed so strange that I was afraid I would either laugh or cry right there in front of everyone. So I discreetly backed out of the room and composed myself in the hallway till at last I heard the organ play the recession, then happy, squealing noises, and chairs moving and the clattering of plates.

As I attempted to steal back in for the eats, I felt a strong hand on my shoulder. Toby Castle's.

"You look lost." She was wearing a tux, expensive and custom-tailored, no rental.

"Just disoriented. I'm supposed to say 'Congratulations' to the groom and 'Best wishes' to the bride. Right?"

"So?"

"So? In this case, which is which?"

"Ah . . . How about a heartfelt 'I'm so happy for you both'? Have some champagne." She handed me an effervescing stem glass. "You want to try for the bouquet?"

"I'm already married."

"But only to a *man*. You may have better luck next time."

"I wish *you* were a man, Toby. You'd be just my type."

As we assailed the buffet table, I noticed a slight change of cast among the resident celebrants.

"I don't see Vera, the runaway mother, and poor little Jonathan."

"They're gone." Toby withdrew a cigar from her breast pocket and rolled it between her fingers. "After we talked last time, I phoned Vera's mother in Michigan and wrung the truth out of her."

"Ah-hah."

"Turned out it wasn't Jonathan's father who was beating up the kid after all." She bit off the end of the cigar, placed it between her lips, and lit it with a wooden match, cupping her hand and taking deep puffs. "It was Vera herself—she's got emotional problems."

"Sorry."

"So now, Jonathan is back with his father, and Vera is locked up for defying a custody order."

"Happy ending."

"It's neither." She led me to a loveseat by the organ. "Because now she wants a lawyer. And she's threatening to turn in everyone who sheltered her along the way and name us all as accessories if we don't raise the money to get her one."

"What a creep."

"Sometimes I'm too close to people to see them clearly."

I bit into a meat pastry and decided it wasn't worth the jaw effort. There were at least two hundred women attached to this organization, and not a one of them could cook worth spit. I put the thing back on my plate for later disposal.

"What happened to pregnant Jenny?"

"She decided to leave."

"Then she must be drunk on her ass somewhere."

"Wrong." Toby had no expression. "She must be sober and locked up in a room on the top floor."

I sat all the way back. "You abrogated her civil rights?"

"Right."

"After that big liberal song and dance about ensuring a mother's control over her own body?"

"I don't want to give the government"—she set her lips—"the *male*-run government that power. But I took it for myself outside the law."

"You'll have to turn the girl loose sometime—"

"After the baby is born healthy."

"—and then she'll go running to the police about false imprisonment."

Toby held her hands out to indicate the present company. "Who will support her story? You?"

"Not I."

"The crisis of prenatal abuse is too big for the government to handle." She puffed on her cigar. "It takes one person."

I rummaged in my purse for the forensic photo. "Now that I have your attention . . ."

"You do."

"Would you look at this?" I held it out. "We've got a face for the hippie in the wall."

She accepted the photo but didn't look until it was at eye level. Then she flinched slightly. "Eric." And handed it back to me. "He was one of the street people."

"What else do you remember about him?"

"He seemed like a decent kid. But then he got one of the girls pregnant and ran out on her, so he must have been a punk."

"But you see, he did not run out."

"Yes. Now I see that."

"Do you recall his having any enemies?"

"You kidding? He wasn't important enough. Just another hippie hanging out, smoking pot, singing peace songs."

"So Ray Lowery offered you information," Frank said. "Deep-six your pet theory that he's the murderer."

"Nah, the guy was just blowing smoke."

I was sitting in the backseat of his unit, glad it was an unmarked one and not a blue and white with a cage and no handles on the rear doors.

"That's *your* reading." Officer Curtis Prout was in the suicide seat holding his Styrofoam coffee cup in both hands. When he opened the door for me, I had noted that his "coffee" looked and smelled a lot like beer. "But Lowery seems serious about getting himself a reward."

"Why not? It would be easy for him to take the money and just give eyewitness evidence against someone who's too dead to contradict him."

Frank rested his pad on the steering wheel. "Like Kathy, the girl who killed herself?"

"Or Clay Shaw, or Ted Bundy. What's he got to lose?"

"I've got a better question," Frank returned. "What did Ray Lowery have to gain from killing Dowd?"

I leaned over the seat back. "Try this. Eric used to sit at the end of the bar near the cash register. Suppose he observed Ray's sticky fingers and threatened to tell the world."

"That would be a motive," Prout admitted. "But Ray Lowery doesn't look like man enough to kill anybody."

"He was in better shape twenty-one years ago."

Prout took another swig of Budweiser coffee. "Consider that the people he was working for are a pretty scary bunch of folks. When a man thinks his life is in danger, he makes that extra effort."

"Women do it for more emotional reasons," Frank said. "For example, suppose a man makes her pregnant and then deserts her, so—"

I cut him off. "Sheila wasn't strong enough."

"Maybe not. And that moves us along to Toby Castle."

"You don't think Eric got *her* pregnant?"

He grimaced to show he got the joke. "Here's a militant feminist, very protective of women. When poor Sheila got in trouble, maybe Castle overheard the man responsible making plans to throw her over and get out of town. She could have got angry enough to put young Dowd in the wall. I'd bet my job she was strong enough."

Prout nodded over his cup. "Toby Castle is strong enough to knock your dick in your watch pocket."

"Strong but gentle," I said. "She wouldn't hurt anyone."

"Anyone *female*," Frank amended. "That Amazon is notorious for fighting our 'patriarchal tyranny.' Do you really think her incapable of murder in defense of an oppressed woman?"

"But she would need a better reason than seduction and an unplanned pregnancy."

"Maybe those would have been reason enough when she was young and hotheaded. Suppose she was in love with Sheila Casey. Is that outside the realm of possibility?"

I recalled the way Toby looked when she said Sheila's name.

"No."

TWENTY-FIVE

Diamond Lil's was as dim and musty as always. The theme from A *Summer Place* was straining the old juke as an undernourished blond shook her bony shoulders in the spotlight, utterly ignored by her audience of two street people. The sallow-faced "audience" had paid only a dollar each for their drinks and were supposed to be acting as shills, but they just slumped over their highballs and made no pretense of being entertained.

The manager seemed not to have moved from his barstool since my last visit. He didn't offer me a job this time; maybe a ray of sunlight had followed me inside to illuminate my level of depreciation.

I asked, "Is Sheila backstage?"

"Nah, she up and quit the other night. Didn't even come by for her last paycheck."

"Do you know where she's staying?"

Sheila Casey lived in the right half of a double shotgun on Decatur Street. Her side of the house was painted, her front window washed and framed with starched curtains. Her front stoop was scrubbed. The left half of the double, by contrast, looked like a slum with flaking paint and a window so dirty it was opaque. The right half had a welcome mat with a picture of a cat on it and a little pearly-white doorbell. I stood on the first and pushed the second. The door opened within seconds.

At first I thought it was a sister or a roommate who had answered the bell. But when she said my name, I realized this was Sheila herself, no longer looking like the girl on the poster. The jilted bride who hadn't allowed herself to change in twenty years had now changed completely overnight.

"You like my hair this way?" It was combed naturally now, not teased. She patted the crown. "I'm letting it grow out. I think I've earned the right to turn gray."

"They told me you quit your job at Diamond Lil's."

"There's no reason to dance anymore."

I took the chintz-covered chair she offered and glanced around for a discreet inventory of her house. As with any shotgun, every room was visible clear through to the rearmost kitchen. The place was cheaply furnished but well kept, featuring plastic-covered lamp shades and the clear, dust-free surfaces of householders who never read.

Commanding the mantel over the gas heater was an eight-by-ten color portrait of Sheila's son in his dress uniform. I sucked in a breath and held it. This was the portrait also of Eric Dowd as I had known him. Yesterday's murdered hippie would live on in today's handsome young soldier.

"Is Keith your only child?"

"Oh, yes. My honey was the first and only boy for me," she admitted softly. "And he said I was almost the first girl for him, too."

"From what I've learned about Eric Dowd, he didn't seem all that innocent."

"Eric? Well, actually, he didn't like his name. He told me to just call him Honey."

I could understand why he didn't want the name anymore,

besmirched as it was. But then why use it at all? Another mystery. I folded my hands in my lap, not to disturb the doilies on the armrests. "What are you going to do now?"

She had just opened her mouth to reply when we were interrupted by the sound of knuckles against the panel of the front door.

"Excuse me. That'll be my friend Jeff Boudreaux." Sheila rose and opened the door to Jeff Boudreaux. "Hi, come in. You remember Cherry? She used to work with me at Madame Julie's."

The caller looked at me shyly and looked away again.

"Uh, maybe. I don't know. Pleased to meet you, ma'am."

Jeff Boudreaux would have fit anyone's stereotype of a "dumb coonass." He was over six feet tall and topped two hundred pounds in his mechanic's uniform with his name embroidered on the pocket. His hands were calloused and stained from twenty years of working in some grease pit.

Not wanting to stick out one of mine, I made a sort of bow.

"Hello, Jeff. Were you around when Sheila started dancing?"

"Yeah. I was always around." He turned to Sheila, or rather, to her shoes. "It's all tuned up for you. Good for another five thousand miles."

"Thank you, hon. I've got your roast on right now." She smiled at me and shrugged. "Jeff and I do favors for each other all the time. I cook; he takes care of my Honda. Will you wait while I fix the hot potato salad?"

"Sure, I'll wait." Jeff watched her scuttle into the kitchen, then settled on the flimsy wingback couch, which sagged under his weight.

"Why not? I been waiting for her since we were . . ." He covered his face with his hands as though the answer were written on his palms. "Twelve. Yeah, that's how long I been loving Sheila. Twenty-seven years."

"Since you were schoolchildren?"

"We got engaged on our high school graduation day, and I gave her a ring." He shifted to thrust a hand into his hip pocket, then brought it out again. "This ring."

"You still have it?"

"Took me fifty weeks to make all the payments."

"If Sheila had a good man like you twenty years ago, what was she doing on Bourbon Street?"

"I never wanted her to take a job. Heck, I was bringing home eighty bucks a week myself then." He polished the stone on his sleeve. "I told her we could make it if we stayed with my ma for a while. But then Sheila said we couldn't get married till we had a place of our own and she'd work a few months to buy the furniture."

"Dancing at Madame Julie's?"

"It paid better than White Castle, she claimed. I was mad, naturally, but I couldn't stay mad at Sheila. She was real special, like a little princess." His eyes were as soft as a Jersey cow's. "We were both saving, and between us we had nearly a thousand dollars for furniture. She was almost ready to quit dancing."

"Then Eric Dowd came along."

"How could I compete with a guy like that?" Jeff looked up at the cracked ceiling. "He was handsome, like Brian Jones, you know? Had this Carnaby Street look with all the fancy clothes."

My eyes stole to the picture on the mantelpiece.

"I remember that he was a cute boy."

"So one night in May, I went by the club as usual to drive her home, and Sheila gave me this ring back. Said she couldn't marry me but she'd always think of me as a friend."

The ring looked tiny in his big, rough hand.

"So you stopped seeing her?"

"No, I kep' on seein' her." The ring went back into his pocket. "Just as a customer, though. Every night, I'd go in the club and buy my drink and leave it sit in front of me while I watched her dance. Then I'd go home. If all she'd let me be was a friend, well, that's all I'd be."

"But why did you hang on so long?"

"We old-fashioned in my family. When we fall in love, that's it." He made a sideways chopping motion.

Twenty-six

Business was slow in Darnold's Doughnut Shop during the supper hour. There were maybe a dozen cops in the place. No more.

I tapped Frank on the shoulder. "I'm back."

"Did you get any more out of the lovelorn Miss Casey?"

"I really don't think she knew any more. But I found out there was another witness on the scene. Sheila had a lifelong admirer, a mechanic named Jeff Boudreaux."

"You mean the late Eric Dowd had a rival?"

"It went deeper than that." I told him the story of Jeff's enduring love for Sheila and his long nights of sitting at the bar in Diamond Lil's with his drink untouched in front of him, watching her dance.

"Is that right?" Frank seemed unaffected by the poignancy of the tale. "Maybe you've got something. Is this Boudreaux strong enough to wall up a hippie?"

"Ten hippies in a stack if he wanted to, but he's a gentle man."

"A man who loves a woman enough to wait twenty-one years for her is pretty drastically involved." Frank used his little wooden coffee stirrer. "So what happens when she tells him she's about to marry another guy? A hippie at that? He goes back to the club. The other guy is there alone, maybe cleaning up. They have words. Boudreaux loses his temper and hits, maybe harder than he meant to. Then he hides the hippie's body so Sheila will think he ran out on her and come back to old faithful."

"But that didn't happen."

"No, because Sheila didn't realize that the man she loved was dead, so she just waited. And Boudreaux couldn't exactly tell her why she was wasting her time, so he had to wait, too."

"Your scenario would make good television, but for some serious miscasting. Jeff is no murderer."

"According to your ladylike opinion, which is losing value by the minute."

"What do you mean by that?"

"Only that." He bit off the words. "You've been holding out on me again, Margo."

"Me? I . . . hey!"

"It was bad enough that you lied about Laura Grant."

"I didn't lie; I just sort of left her out."

"But now it just happened to slip your mind that Don Fortunado was slinking around while all this was going on. Back then he was the mob's bagman."

"Robert would just came in once a week to make collections. He had no contact with Eric."

"How do you know?"

When I got back in my car, I flicked on the dome light and made a neat list of suspects, writing: Ray Lowery, Jim Turner, Jeff Boudreaux. (That one was just to be thorough. I *knew he* didn't do it.) I continued to be thorough with the names Sheila Casey, Laura Grant, Rocco Fortunado, Rev. Reggie, Toby, and Samantha. Then I just stared blankly at the list like it was the final exam for a class I'd never attended.

Not one of these people had the three requisite elements of

a killer: a proven motive, plus the opportunity, plus the ability.

"Mrs. Fortier?" asked the pointed little face. "I'm Andy Norgaard from *Southern Lavender*."

I usually say, "Ooh, *do* call me *Margo*," but the winsome creature on the front porch looked callow enough to be my son, so I figured that "Mrs. Fortier" was the appropriate address in his case.

Andy Norgaard was a slight young man with a white eelskin briefcase and three earrings in one ear and looked as though he had never shaved or had to.

"I *love* your decor. What an exquisite use of color and pattern!"

"My husband picked out everything."

"I don't doubt it."

He followed me into the living room and sat himself on the couch daintily, with his knees tight together, which I should probably learn to do.

"Thank you so much for giving me this time, Mrs. Fortier." He took out a tape recorder and placed it between us on the coffee table. "I know you must be busy, juggling marriage and career."

"Oh, but there's no juggling involved." I arranged myself in the armchair and waved a hand gracefully to show the manicure. "My marriage is *good* for my career. Julian is very supportive."

"Yes, and that aspect is especially interesting to us." Young master Norgaard simpered and tapped his smooth chin. "Considering that your husband is the most distinguished closeted gay in the city."

"I . . . Upf! . . . Hanh?"

"In fact, we were hoping that he would honor us by celebrating his sexuality officially in *Southern Lavender*."

"Wha . . . " I felt as though I'd just got slapped in the face with a mop. As soon as my breath returned, I hollered for help. "Julian!"

"I heard" came from the other side of the pocket doors. Then in one movement, my gallant husband pulled them open and emerged from the library where, I realized, he must have been listening all the time. "What is this garbage?"

"Ooh, Mr. *Fortier.*" Norgaard fluttered to his feet and held out his soft white hand, which dangled, ignored. "We're beginning a unique new feature in our magazine. We call it 'I'm Coming Out!'"

Julian looked dumbfounded. "Who's coming out?"

"A different person each month." Andy bobbed with enthusiasm. "In every issue someone very important is going to announce to the world that he's one of us. And I would like to invite *you* to be the *first.*"

"Are you loony?" Julian was as loud as I'd ever heard him. "I can't do any such thing. I have an important image in this community."

"Exactly why you should, Mr. Fortier. Don't you see, you are important as a role model for young gays."

"I am no role model. I'm a private citizen whom the Supreme Court legally endows with the right to be let alone."

Andy shook his impertinent little head, side to side, ticktock, ticktock. "Excuse me, sir, but you can't claim 'right to privacy.' As the president and spokesmen for the French Landmark Society, you are quite a public person. And your wife, the society columnist"—he lifted a hand shoulder-high and pointed at me—"is famous, too."

I said, "For *this* I'm famous?"

Andy went on without me. "We have got to stop being furtive as though our lifestyle were something *shame*ful." He posed with a finger against his hollow chest. "*I* have never hidden the fact that I'm gay."

I erupted. "As if you *could* have." (The little jerk swished like a feather duster.)

"It's okay, Margo. I'll handle this."

"Mr. Fortier, haven't you heard of the latest rash of fag bashings? The skinheads have an open season on us."

"It's not happening here in New Orleans."

"Not yet, but they're gaining. We get more popular as targets every day."

"Then all your magazine does is make us *bigger* targets. That's no answer."

"The answer is in recognition by the mainstream of society, and we won't get that until they realize how many of us there *are*. I say stand up and be counted. Be *proud* you're gay."

Julian threw up his hands. "I can't be *proud* I'm gay as though it were something I'd striven for and achieved. I was *born* this way."

Andy drew himself up to his full shrimpy height for a lofty pronouncement.

"I thought it was only fair to inform you that you will be mentioned in our next issue, which comes out a week from today." He pulled a magazine from his eel-skin briefcase as though presenting arms. "Here is an advance copy."

The page was already turned to the "Take Them for an Outing" column, and the first entry in boldface hit me right in the eye.

"History maven Julian Fortier is closemouthed about his own sexual history. Oh, don't be so modest, dearie."

I handed the magazine over to Julian without daring to comment. He read the item, moving his lips with the words, then his jaw dropped, and so did the magazine, which Andy hustled to catch in midair. "My sexual history is entirely my *own* business. And what's a 'maven'?"

"Don't worry, Mr. Fortier. The people who admire you may be shocked at first. But then they'll start thinking, 'Well, if a wonderful person like *him* is one of them, they can't all be so bad.' "

"The best club in the city would blackball me!"

The little slut took a righteous tone. "It's not a club worth belonging to if they only let uptight *straight* people in."

"Heavens no," Julian waved him off. "We're of all persuasions. At least three of the governing committee are gay that I know of. One vice president dresses up in women's clothes. And there are two foot fetishists and a masochist. But they don't go on 'Geraldo' about it, for pity's sake!"

"Everyone in life has to stand up for something."

"Certainly, I'm willing to stand up for something," Julian returned. "But I want to *choose* what I stand up for. The cause of gay rights shouldn't be forced on me just because I'm gay myself. I leave that to others."

Norgaard's little snout went up. "You're involved whether you want to be or not."

"Only in my private life."

"Privacy ends where hypocrisy begins."

"But I'm *not* a hypocrite."

"Oh no? You've been living a lie for a lot of years." Norgaard looked at me as though I were a nasty exhibit. "Pretending to be heterosexual."

"Why not?" I went for his scrawny throat. *"You're pretending to be human."*

I would have throttled the little snake, but Julian intercepted, catching my arms and whirling me around all in one graceful motion. "Mr. Norgaard? I'm sure you have important business elsewhere."

"Don't worry, I'm leaving," the little ferret said. "I just wanted to give you a chance to walk out of the closet yourself, with head held high, before the issue appears. It will be up to you."

And having said that, Andy Norgaard picked up his briefcase, turned heel, and flounced through the hallway and out the front door.

"Oh, Margo!" Julian collapsed on the couch, in stages like an old building being dynamited. "How can they say that about me?"

I patted his shoulder. "Relax, Neg. 'Maven' is just a Yiddish word that means, like, 'expert.'"

"Then I don't mind the 'maven' part. But, Lord, if my sex life ever becomes common knowledge . . . " He wrung his hands. "I won't even be able to get into the *Hair* Club."

"Andy said the magazine won't be on the stands till next week." I hurried to my Rolodex and started rolling. "I'll make an appointment with Mickey. We'll go see what your legal rights are."

TWENTY-SEVEN

Mickey Monaghan, Esq., looked down to read the *Southern Lavender* item through the lower lens on his bifocals. Then he closed the magazine and took off his glasses. "So Julian's being outed."

"That's why we're here, Mick. Now, is there any way we can stop them from publishing it?"

I did the talking for both of us while Julian did the head shaking and hand-wringing.

"You mean prior restraint?" Our attorney curled his lips around the term. "Unless you can prove a threat to national security, we'd never get it. You'd have to wait till after it's published, then sue for libel, but . . ."

"But what?"

"But there are two things wrong with that. First, truth is the best defense for a libel suit. Julian would have to prove in a court of law that he's *not* gay. Want to try?"

"Very funny," Julian muttered.

"Then even supposing he were believed. A vehement denial of the charge implies that there is something inherently odious and disgraceful about being homosexual." He smiled slightly. "That would alienate roughly half the people in the city. And then try to prove that the imputation has damaged him materially."

"*Damaged* me? It would make my work *impossible.*" Julian raked his hair. "Do you realize that I'd be branded for the rest of my life? I couldn't even go into high schools anymore to tell kids about their heritage. They'd think I was there to proselytize for the gay lifestyle."

I put my hand on his shoulder and squeezed it.

"What can we do, Mick?"

"You can forget it is what you can do." Mickey slapped the magazine down on his desk. "Who reads this rag, anyway? A few thousand homosexuals? If I were you, I'd ignore this shit. Next month there will be a whole new set of names in their crappy column."

"You're saying we should just brazen it out?"

"Or maybe counter their propaganda with some of your own." He put his glasses back on and looked me up and down. "For example, Margo, have you considered getting pregnant?"

It wasn't even funny.

"At this point, I couldn't get pregnant in the Iberville Project on Saturday night."

"All dried up?"

"*Matured!*"

"Then at least you two can get seen around town engaging in wholesome, 'mature' family-type activities."

"You mean Mr. and Mrs. Julian Fortier as interpreted by Norman Rockwell?"

"You've got it. We're talking a reaffirmation of traditional values here."

February 21, 1991

The long-awaited ground war seems imminent. Hussein responded to Bush's "Get outta town by noon" ultimatum by ordering his troops to detonate the charges set around Kuwaiti oil wells. We hear that one-quarter of the country's oil fields have now been sabotaged and occupying Iraqi soldiers are executing citizens by the thousands.

Fred Francis on NBC reported that the frontline Iraqi soldiers were living on four tablespoons of rice a day. The cannon fodder at the end of their supply line have been pinned down in trenches for weeks and are out of food, water, and fuel.

"But one thing most of them *do* have is a nice clean white surrender flag somewhere on their person."

Francis pulled out his own handkerchief and waved it in illustration.

Our pilots drop leaflets with cartoon illustrations instructing soldiers how to defect, and Iraqis are flocking to turn themselves in, clutching the leaflets in their fists.

Bush delivered a brief exhortation of patriotism with his characteristic fractured syntax, and, as usual, I thought I was listening to Dana Carvey.

Hussein is throwing even more bombs at Israel to pull them into the battle, not minding that they're just innocent bystanders.

During a concert by the Israeli Philharmonic in Tel Aviv, the air raid sirens went off, signaling yet another SCUD attack, and the conductor, Zubin Mehta, had the entire orchestra withdraw to safer ground. But a few minutes later, the seventy-one-year-old Isaac Stern walked out onto the bare stage and finished the program all by himself, rendering his violin solos as sweetly as though he were playing at the gate to heaven. The entire audience, wearing their gas masks, stayed to listen.

I reaffirmed that I basically like Jews.

February 22, 1991

Julian was chuckling at the TV screen. "I'm watching the news on Univision."

"What for? It isn't even in English."

"Exactly the point. You get the non-Anglo view of events. Listen to this: José Gray just said, 'Saddam Hussein promised that the ground war would be 'the Mother of All Battles,' but at this moment the Iraqi soldiers don't wish to be its children.'"

"He said that, did he?"

"I guess it's funnier in Spanish."

"It must be."

"Do you want to watch the war?"

"No thanks."

"It's getting good."

"Cripe, if John Wayne hadn't died, we wouldn't need this war."

But there was nothing better to do on a Sunday afternoon, so I dragged my armchair over next to his.

The networks kept repeating the pool footage of a wretched half-naked and starving Iraqi soldier who had just been taken prisoner. In great relief, he leaned on the shoulders of two of his captors and kissed one on the cheek.

I wanted to shout, *"Feed* that poor man."

Julian used his remote to turn down the sound.

"Haven't you noticed an Aquarian age humanity in the conduct of this war?"

"You mean the surgical strikes at strictly military targets."

"Exactly. Here we are trying to spare enemy civilians as though they were our own. *Newsweek* actually ran a poll asking if we should stop the air war because it's doing too much damage to Iraq and its civilians." He punched the channel selector back up to Univision. "During the second world war, did we worry about civilian lives in Berlin? Would Hitler have expected us to?"

I said, "All we knew about the Germans were from the propaganda films. They were all steely-eyed Nazis. But now we watch the Iraqis every night on CNN. It's hard to think of people as faceless monsters when you see them in hospital beds with their limbs shot off."

"That's exactly why Saddam has let the newsmen stay in Baghdad. He stuffed a command center with innocent women and children, then when we bombed the daylights out of it, he claimed we were inhuman monsters for targeting a 'civilian bomb shelter.'"

"He still hasn't explained why a 'civilian bomb shelter' had a twelve-foot barbed-wire fence and a secret basement full of communications equipment."

"True." Julian pushed up the volume for "Noticiero." "But he knows we care about those women and children, so he's used our weakness against us."

"That's great propaganda for the hawks. More proof the guy is so devilishly evil that he has to be stopped before he gets nuclear weapons and takes over the world."

Hussein is much easier to hate than Ho Chi Minh, who seemed a vague Confucian figure back then. Ho had way too much dignity to pat the heads of hostage children for video cameras.

Julian pointed as General Schwarzkopf's friendly face filled the TV screen and he delivered his candid assessment of Saddam Hussein.

"He is neither a strategist, nor is he schooled in the operational art, nor is he a tactician, nor is he a general, nor is he a soldier. Other than that, he's a great military man."

I laughed and prodded Julian. "Isn't Stormin' Norman neat? I could get a real case on him."

"I wonder if he's related to Willard Scott."

The newscast wound up with a family segment as a matronly counselor advised us, "How to warn your children about drugs on the streets."

When I was a kid, it was just "Look both ways before crossing."

Twenty-eight

As I jogged past the doorway on Montegut, there was no sign of the young couple. Maybe they had folded up their blanket and gone back to college.

In their place now sat an old man, thin and raggedy, a typical derelict. I decided the couple must have sublet.

It was after six, and night had fallen early. It was already too dark to be out jogging.

The trash was due for pickup the next morning, so rusting refuse cans lined the sidewalk and piles of bulging green plastic bags were arranged around telephone poles. I passed the corner of Spain Street, where an ugly stray hound, gray with black spots, rooted through the garbage for its dinner. The dog had torn open the most promising bag with the efficiency of long practice and was devouring a tangle of chicken bones in choking gulps before the householder could see the mess through the window and drive it away. The spotted hound was thin and sharp-boned with a dull, ragged coat, so I guessed it had been abandoned long ago and learned to survive the hard way, hiding from the dogcatcher by day under some vacant house, then stealing out after dark to forage for scraps.

A black youth sauntered toward me now looking too nonchalant, and practicing my usual city savvy, I crossed the empty street to avoid him. That's when I saw another of the same type standing there in the shadow of a bush, watching. I reeled around and started back the way I came, then heard a whistled signal behind me, and running footsteps. The punks had dropped their pose as harmless evening strollers and were chasing me all out.

Now, I revved up and ran down the street like "Middle-Aged Man," drawing on all of my jogger's aerobic capacity. I'd have bet the punks were sprinters with no staying power and in a long-distance run, I could have beat them both. But, hell, they only had to run long enough to catch me, which they were sure to do in about forty seconds.

And there was no soul in sight, on the street or through any lighted window to call for help. Only the stray hound was still on the corner, licking up the remains of its scrounged meal.

So I stopped short, found enough breath in my lungs to whistle hard, then hollered, "Here, Brutus!" and slapped my knees. The dog looked up, puzzled. I whistled again. "C'mon, boy. Let's go *home!*"

This wretched-looking cur probably hadn't been summoned by a human in months and was overjoyed at the attention. It came like a shot, bounding as excitedly as a puppy to meet me. It was all over me then, panting and sloshing my face. When I dared to look around again, the punks had disappeared. My ruse had worked. Most blacks in New Orleans are deathly afraid of dogs, so even this sorry specimen could lend the image of a protector.

I let it walk me all the way home, then not until we reached the safety of my front porch did I realize that Brutus was a bitch.

"Hold it right there," I advised her. "I'm going to pay you."

The hound wagged uncertainly but waited as I unlocked my doors. I walked through the house to the kitchen, unwrapped a soup bone I'd been saving, and brought it back out to her.

"Here's some real ham with the meat still on it. Not bad for a few minutes work, right?"

I put it down on the flagstone path. She sniffed the bone but then just left where it lay and wagged expectantly.

"No, you can't stay here. I can't keep a dog, see?" She didn't understand, so I pushed her away. "Just take your bone and go, all right?" I returned to the house and locked the iron gate behind me without looking back. Hidden in the dark of my living room, I peeked through the blinds, and the hound was still sitting there, staring at my front door.

She would get tired of waiting and be gone by morning.

Before the dogcatchers came around in their white vans.

Fifteen minutes later, I heard Julian's steps on the porch and hurried to unlock the inside door for him. He hurried past me, quickly shrugged out of his coat, and hung it on the rack.

"You know what?" His voice was high and strained. "I ran into Arnie Raisch downtown. Remember, he was best man at our wedding."

"Best singer, too." The highlight of the event had been Arnie's singing "Oh Promise Me" like the first tenor in a choir of angels. "How is he?"

Nuts! I shouldn't have asked.

Julian went straight back to the bar in the living room and poured a shot of brandy before answering.

"He's lost about fifty pounds. How do you think he is?"

"He's got it, too, then?"

"Yeah, he's got it, too."

Appearing soon: another sidewalk sale in Faubourg Marigny.

"I'm sorry, Julian. That's the fifth friend we've heard about just since Christmas."

He pushed his fingers through his hair so that it stood up.

"Wake me from this nightmare." He knocked back the

brandy in two swallows. "We live in an age where premeditated murder rates a year in jail and sleeping with the wrong person incurs the death penalty."

"I'm just grateful that *you're* healthy."

"Am I healthy, though?"

"You always test negative."

"But everyone I know is either positive or hiding from the truth by not being tested at all. Gays are like canaries in a mine shaft! Whenever there's a new epidemic, we call attention to the problem by keeling over dead!" He paced the room, squeezing the glass almost hard enough to crush it. "It looks like I'm going to be the last one alive in the whole damned *region*."

"They're bound to find a cure before long."

"Oh, I'm sure of it. The 'cure' will be that everybody who has it will die, and then it will be gone." He returned to the bar and reached for the Moselle this time, pouring it into a stem glass on automatic. "Could that creep Andy be right? Sometimes I feel like a Jew who converted to Christianity just to escape the Inquisition. Here I am safely married to you."

"You feel guilty about choosing a normal home life?"

"Maybe about living a lie."

"But you're not lying, Julian. You just gave up something you wanted for something else you wanted more. It was a hard decision, not an immoral one."

"Thanks, Margo . . . I want to believe you." He circled the rug twice more, then carried his glass over to the window and pulled the curtain aside. "There's something funny. As I was coming in, I saw this hound sitting out there on the front walk, and it's still there."

"She is? Oh, bother!"

"You know her?"

"She saved me from muggers tonight and walked me home." I joined Julian at the window and kept talking, grateful at least for the change of topic. "So I paid the mutt off with a soup bone and told her to scram."

"But she's not a mutt; she's purebred Catahoula."

"Cata-what?"

"The Catahoula is the only dog breed developed here in Louisiana. It has a great nose for tracking rabbits through the swamps."

"Nose or not, I can't believe they'd deliberately breed an animal to be that ugly."

He sipped thoughtfully.

"It would be nice to have a dog around the house. There's no better burglar alarm."

"Maybe. But if I get us a dog, it will be a strong handsome young boxer, or a bullmastiff. Not a scroungy old thing like that. I'd be ashamed of her."

"I agree that she's scroungy. But . . . who knows? A few good meals and a bath might change that. From what I can see, your savior has pretty good bloodlines. Nice markings."

"Great. Then maybe some rabbit hunter will come along and take her home."

"I'm sure. There must be scads of those in the Ninth Ward."

Twenty-Nine

February 23, 1991

I got out our company china and set the table according to Amy Vanderbilt's diagram. I bought her big red etiquette book when I started studying manners back around '75 and still have to resort to it about once a month. The salad fork, dinner fork, and dessert fork were lined up like soldiers.

Our sterling flatware are monogrammed with an F as though they were Fortier heirlooms, but of course I'd bought the set myself. It was Julian's assignment to pick out the pattern, as he has all the taste in the family.

An arrangement of winter flowers was set off side so as not to block anyone's view during our tasteful chitchat.

Invitations to our dinner parties are coveted in some circles. Social climbers want to come because we're Fortiers, real people because the host is one fantastic cook. Two weeks of Julian's year abroad were spent at the Cordon Bleu school in Paris. But such talent as his can't be learned. You have to be French to begin with, and then it's bred in the genes.

I stepped out on the porch to light our gas lamp, and my next-door neighbor was out walking her cat with a leash and collar.

I waved. "Evenin', Ida."

"See you got a dog," she called back to me.

"How's that? Nuts!" Sure enough, the wretched hound was still sitting there in front of the house.

"Oh no! That . . . " I flicked a hand. "Just a stray."

"She thinks she's yours. Doesn't look like she's moved from that spot all day, even to eat."

"I'm not paying attention to her. She'll go away."

I went into the kitchen and got some of Julian's leftover rice and gravy, shoveled a heap of it onto a disposable aluminum tray, and carried it back outside to the Catahoula. But I didn't look at her because I didn't want to encourage her to hang around.

I didn't want her to starve, either. She deserved better than that.

Our first guest to arrive was Gaby Schindler. She's on my A-list, always invited. I helped her off with her jaguar coat. Which she doesn't feel guilty about wearing because when she bought it, the jaguar wasn't endangered yet.

Probably the *dinosaur* wasn't endangered yet.

"Your dress iss *marvelous*, darling. I alvays luff dat one."

"Always? Are you implying that it's kind of old?"

"All der calf-length skirts are old now. De minis haf come back."

"Not to my house they haven't. I didn't even look good in them last time around."

One favorable aspect of midlife is that now I'm free to keep the unsightly parts covered. There will be no more cavorting on beaches in my skimpies or undressing at picnics for casual friends. Fortunately, men my age prefer bright conversation and dim lighting.

Gaby indicated her own hem, which covered the knee exactly.

"Dis style never changes."

"All styles change. The only thing that changes faster is style *setters*."

Scant months ago, the Bardot-type Claudia Schiffer was

featured in all the Guess? ads. Now their print model is a dark girl with sixties-look eyeliner. No sooner do I learn a model's name than she vanishes from the scene.

"You may be right, my dear. Now, I'll take my usual place at de table and my usual drink."

"Right this way, Gaby. I've got your martini ready to pour. After all, I wasn't a barmaid for nothing."

Julian cooks; I mix and shake.

Toby Castle came to dinner stag and looked stunning in a black velvet dinner jacket and gray paisley vest.

I took her silver-handled cane. "Thank you so much for coming."

"Wouldn't miss it." She bowed solemnly. "I look on this as a sociological excursion into the privileged class."

"You're one of the privileged tonight. Here's your black Russian."

"You remembered from the old days." She sipped and smiled. "Fabulous."

"It's the vodka. We Irish have a way with potatoes."

"I'm sure. Say, I noticed the interesting dog you have out there."

"Ycch, that poor creature's not ours. I'm just letting her hang around till someone comes to claim her."

"Don't go without bathing till someone comes to claim her."

Lieutenant and Mrs. Frank Washington were exactly on time. Frank isn't what you'd call a bundle of personality, but his wife, Chloe, is an asset to any group. She looks like Phylicia Rashad and has great style and wit.

I mixed an expert whiskey sour for her and a Gibson for him.

Julian placed a basket of hot homemade bread table center.

"We have real butter and also that other stuff, I Wish It Were Butter or Too Bad It's Not Butter, whatever they call it."

I said, "I remember when butter used to be called 'the

seventy-cent spread.' Now *margarine* is 'the seventy-cent spread.'"

"Is this a denouement dinner?" Chloe asked as she took her chair. "I know you and Frank are working on a murder mystery. Have you brought all the suspects together tonight so you can point the finger of judgment over dessert?"

Frank glanced around the dining room. "I'm afraid we lack the full complement. My own favorite candidate is one Robert Fortunado, who hasn't made an appearance."

"I forgot to put his invitation in the mail," Julian said dryly.

"Officer Prout thinks the murderer is the jealous rival, Jeff Boudreaux, and I notice he isn't present, either." Frank raised an eyebrow. "But perhaps a mechanic doesn't quite fit in with the Fortier milieu."

"It isn't that," I defended. "Jeff just wouldn't feel comfortable here. Besides, I don't suspect him for a minute."

"And of course you don't suspect Laura Pennyson Grant, either."

"Now, *there's* someone who doesn't fit in." Julian placed the decanted wine at the head of the table. "I'm not about to cook for a debutante. They don't eat."

"Besides," I said, "we know Laura wasn't physically able to carry an adult male, dead or alive."

"I agree with you," the lieutenant agreed with me. "Reverend Reggie McCann, by contrast, was well able."

"I invited him to dinner, but he's busy preaching tonight."

"So the only actual suspect present for the evening's denouement is . . . " Frank raised his cocktail glass. "Your friend Ms. Castle."

Toby raised her own glass back at him. "I don't mind being a suspect. But find me a decent motive, please."

"I'm working on it." Frank shifted in his chair. "Margo's own suspects are Ray Lowery and Jim Turner, and she's failed to invite either."

"I wouldn't invite those cruds to a *sewer* excavation."

"But I think maybe you're looking down the wrong sewer."

Chloe waggled her salad fork at me. "I see Jim Turner hawking his practice on television, and he looks too wimpy to murder anyone."

"No, he can't be as wimpy as he looks. There was this crip—I mean handicapped veteran in his law office, Jack Gilley. He told me Turner did a righteous lot of killing during the war."

"Margo," Julian chided. "It's no longer politically correct to say 'handicapped.' You have to say 'disabled.' "

"You're both wrong," Toby intervened. "The PC for handicapped is 'physically challenged.' "

"Derelicts are now 'homeless people,' " Frank took a piece of hot bread. "And I found out you can't call those people in *Dances with Wolves* 'Indians' anymore. The politically correct say 'Native Americans.' "

"But we're *all* 'native Americans.' " Julian began ladling the oyster soup into china bowls. "Anyone born somewhere is a native of that place."

Gaby said, "I thought dey called *demselves* 'Indians.' "

"It used to be correct." I passed her a bowl. "And I remember when it was okay to say 'colored people.' " I looked around the table. "As in the National Association for the Advancement of . . . "

Julian put down the ladle. "But we're *all* colored." He ran a finger along the back of his hand. "I mean, we're not transparent."

Chloe said, "I can't keep up myself. I think we're African American now, aren't we dear?"

"Hardly." Frank leaned away from the steaming soup. "General Colin Powell is African American. You and I are just black."

Julian said, "I used to be a fairy. Now I have a 'nontraditional sexual orientation.' "

I waited for Gaby to start in on her soup, then mimicked her, moving the spoon away from me across the bowl instead of toward me, which would be much more sensible but not ladylike.

Then I said, "I love being called a girl, but now I'm supposed to be insulted about it."

"A compliment to your looks, an insult to your status," Chloe offered. "Do you know it's demeaning to call your cat a 'pet.' Now it's an 'animal companion.' "

"You're kidding about that one."

"No I'm not. Ask Cleveland Amory."

Toby buttered her croissant with the real cow product. "What are we supposed to call a Jew these days?"

" 'Old Testament man,' " Julian said without hesitation.

"One of the 'Chosen People,' " Chloe suggested.

"I'd say a 'person of the Hebrew persuasion,' " offered her husband.

"None of the above," I announced to the table. "You're supposed to pretend you don't *notice* he's Jewish, and then when he says he is, you act pleasantly surprised. Remember when we all used to call policemen 'pigs'?"

"I probably did myself," Frank admitted. "Now I see the other side of it."

"I'm sure you do. Who has more heartfelt sympathy for the trials of a cop's life than the cop himself?"

"The cop's *wife*," Chloe intervened. "I know what my husband goes through and for how little. It's unconscionable. Just to think a patrolman gets eighteen thousand a year to risk his life dealing with dangerous sickos, while a sicko writer like Bret Easton Ellis makes three hundred thousand dollars polluting the world with his sadistic fantasies."

Gaby shrugged. "Dat book vill be a best-seller, you vill see. Poor Salman Rushdie had to get a price on hiss head to make so much publicity."

Julian lifted our crawfish phyllos from the server to table center.

"So what is *American Psycho* but an upscale promotion of

the same values expressed by 2 Live Crew? The rape, murder, and mutilation of women."

Chloe accepted a phyllo. "I'm against censorship, but there should be some standard of decency at the record company or the publishing house. I'd like to see what kind of depraved editor it took to accept *American Psycho*."

"Never mind the *editor*," I countered. "I'd like to see the author's *mother*. What kind of woman could have spawned such a pervert?"

"Don't blame the women." Toby helped herself to the broccoli in béarnaise sauce. "Men are responsible for ninety-six percent of the violence in the world. So long as we have men, you can expect glorified murder on a grand scale."

I swallowed a bite of crawfish in thin pastry. "Moving on to the lighter subject of the war, did you hear about Baghdad Betty? She plays records and broadcasts demoralizing propaganda to our troops."

Gaby cocked her head. "You mean like Tokyo Rose?"

"That's the idea, only this chick isn't quite hip. She tells the soldiers, 'While you're fighting over here, your wives and girlfriends are sleeping with Tom Selleck and Bart Simpson!'"

Julian used his tongs on the vegetable plate. "She's out of it. Bart Simpson I can understand. But Selleck was mid-eighties."

Frank asked, "Whom do the women want to sleep with now? Tom Cruise?"

"No, he was three years ago," Julian said. As if he knew.

Gaby chewed carefully and swallowed before venturing, "Mel Geebson would bee nice."

I held up my fork. "Me, Patrick Swayze. A straight guy who can dance. Yum-yum."

Chloe nudged me. "What about Willie Nelson? He can do it for nine hours including a back flip."

I said, "I *adore* Willie Nelson. I'd give him three hours. No back flip."

Frank addressed his plate. "He's bankrupt."

"Then I'd have to feed him first. Two hours, no back flip."

"Absolutely *not*." Julian threw up his hands. "I am *not* going to march into that kitchen and cook for Willie Nelson just so he can get up the strength to pound you for two hours!"

I said, "Why not? You cook for our other guests. You just want to deprive me of some harmless diversion."

"She's right," Chloe said. "You're being unreasonable, Julian."

Toby stroked her chin. "I could take an interest in Julia Roberts from *Pretty Woman*. On second thought, make that Julia Roberts's body double from *Pretty Woman*."

Frank spoke to his lapel. I think only I heard him. "Jasmine Guy."

Our host stood up and filled the empty wineglasses. "It may be possible for all of you to meet your dream dates if, as they say, there are just six degrees of separation between you and anyone else in the country."

"I've heard of dat." Gaby's emeralds flashed. "But I don't understand, Julian. Explain de ting to me."

"It's the theory that someone you know knows someone who knows someone who knows someone who knows someone who knows anyone you can name."

"But I could not be only six degrees separated from Mel Geebson."

"Sure you are," I told her. "You know me; I know Millie at the paper. She interviewed Joan Rivers, who had Jan Hooks on her program, who worked with Mel Gibson on 'Saturday Night Live.' Voilà!"

Frank twitched his mustache. "What about me and Bill Cosby?"

"That's even easier. You know the police chief who knows the governor who knows President Bush who has invited Cosby to the White House."

Chloe wrinkled her nose. "He just wants Cosby to introduce him to Jasmine Guy."

Julian said, "The catch is that you couldn't follow that network down because you don't have lists of all your acquaintances' acquaintances on through to the sixth power."

Then we all stopped speaking at once, perhaps to mentally trace down networks.

In that first whole second of silence there sounded the ultimate evening wrecker, the unmistakable tone: "Reeeeeeeeee."

"Whose beeper iss dat?" Gaby asked. "Margo?"

"You kidding? Since when does a gossip columnist need to be beeped?"

"Maybe Zella Funck's art show has been raided," Julian suggested. "I guarantee it's not for me. My old landmarks aren't going anywhere. Toby?"

She shook her head. "It would take a full-scale SCUD attack to upset that fortress of mine. Chloe?"

"No way. I get only two free nights a year, and this is definitely one of them. Frank?"

"Yes, of course it's for me," her husband allowed glumly. "It's always for me." He pulled his beeper out of an inside pocket, read the phone number at arm's length, and sighed. "Guess what? It's not Jasmine Guy."

Frank hoisted himself up out of his chair and went to the phone in the alcove. He was back at the table in less than a minute, but not to return to his seat. "Bad news for you, Margo. You've lost your favorite suspect in the hippie murder."

"Don't tell me."

"They just found Ray Lowery's body on Almonaster Street. You know how some people dump their trash there? Broken refrigerators? Old mattresses? Dead animals?"

"Ecology outlaws," Chloe volunteered. "They make sure no one's around to get the license number, then throw their garbage out the car door."

"Well, that's where Lowery was found, along the side of the road."

"With the *rest* of the garbage," I said in a witty aside. "For him, I don't care, but that complicates my plan to trick a confession out of the creep."

"It would seem the murderer of the hippie has just claimed another victim. The good news is that I'd rather investigate a recent homicide than an ancient one." Frank reached over to his plate and took an asparagus spear for the road. "I've got to go to work. Please carry on as though I were still here."

Chloe didn't look up from her phyllo. "Not on your life. I'm going to have *fun* now."

Thirty

February 24, 1991

Julian looked up from his *Newsweek*.

"Hello? What are you doing up so early? It isn't even noon yet."

"I know, but I'm hot on this story, after all. I have to meet Frank at one P.M."

"I had an interesting morning myself. I just washed the Catahoula."

"Why?"

"The poor thing was dirty and full of fleas."

"Obviously, Julian, but she isn't our dog."

"I thought maybe after a good wash someone would find her attractive enough to take her home."

"There isn't that much soap in the world, but I appreciate the effort."

"Maybe Lowery did have a motive." Frank was putting on his I'm-trying-to-be-patient voice. "But if *he* killed Dowd, then who killed *him?*"

I sat across from his desk in the cheap chair of molded plastic.

"What makes you sure the murders were related? Suppose

Ray was just killed like everybody else in New Orleans gets killed? Wrong place, wrong time."

"Nobody gets mugged in the Almonaster dump."

"So he was killed somewhere else and carried there."

"Why? Why the freight service for an ordinary mugging?"

"Neatness?"

"Pull up your socks, Margo."

"But this supports my theory that the perp was male."

"So think about the men in the case. Sheila Casey's boyfriend, Jeff Boudreaux, had a motive."

"But he was too nice."

Frank straightened a stack of index cards by knocking them against the edge of his desk.

"I'm sure we can run the criminal courts on your opinions. You'll just sit on the dock and say, 'Nice,' 'Not nice,' as the defendants parade by."

I looked out the window and across the courtyard to Parish Prison. "It would be an improvement on the current system."

"Maybe. Now, let's consider Robert Fortunado. Definitely *not* 'too nice.' "

"But he didn't have a motive either."

"That we *know* about. And your macho friend Toby Castle, though not technically a man . . ."

"I'll concede that she was strong enough. But her motive wasn't." I snapped my fingers. "So it had to be Jim Turner."

"He couldn't have the remotest reason."

"I'd give him the same motive as Ray. Suppose Eric caught *Jim* stealing and threatened to tell."

"But a doorman doesn't handle money. So what's he going to steal? The doorknob? Come on, Margo."

"Okay then. What if there was a fight between Turner and Dowd and Ray remembered?"

"It couldn't have been Turner for this one." Frank tapped a pile of fan-feed computer paper. "The ME says Lowery was hit on the head at least three times, and only one of the blows was fatal."

"So?"

"So, Jim Turner wouldn't have done such a sloppy job. A soldier is trained to kill with silent efficiency."

"He can afford a hitter."

"A contract killer who whomps the mark three times with a tire iron?" Frank looked at me sideways. "I guess he's supposed to be working cheap while he saves up for a gun."

"There are plenty of amateurs out there who would kill their mothers for a bag of crack."

"If this one were an amateur, we'd never find him unless he brags to his confreres. Anyway, you want the perp to be Turner just because you hate lawyers."

"And you want it to be Rocco Fortunado just because you hate gangsters."

"I admit to a prejudice."

Sheila must not have found a job yet. She was home when I called and apparently bored enough to welcome a return visit.

"Hi, Cherry. I made some coffee."

"No thank you." We sat together on the couch. "Did you hear that Ray Lowery is dead?"

"Oh, him? Yes, it was on Channel Four. Would you like a cold drink?"

"I just had one. The cops believe Ray was murdered by the same guy who killed Eric."

"After twenty-one years? But why?"

"Because maybe Ray knew something about the murder at Madame Julie's. You were on the street all those years. Did you ever hear any hint about it?"

"I didn't hang out," she said dully. "I just went to work and went home."

I believed her. Believed that she had never allowed herself any gaiety at all.

I said, "It must be wonderful to have Jeff to look after you."

"Yeah, I guess so. I never thought about it. He's just Jeff, you know?"

"That's the way it is?" I clapped my hands in girlish glee. "Great! Listen, Sheila, I have this girlfriend, Helen, who's single and looking for a nice guy." I took a confidential tone. "I told her about Jeff, and now she's dying to meet him. Would you mind if I fixed them up?"

Sheila looked startled. "Fix them up?"

"Don't worry, I'm sure he'd like Helen. She's very pretty. What's more, she can cook."

Sheila drew her shoulders up. "Well, so can I."

"But Helen's only twenty-five, and she really digs big, rugged men like Jeff. She'll eat him right up." I reached into my purse for a pen and pad. "So let me have Jeff's number, okay? And we'll just get them together and let nature take its course."

Sheila folded her hands tightly. "I'll have to think about that."

"Very well, then." I unclicked my pen. "But please get that number to me as soon as you can. Helen is always whining that this town has about fifty pretty girls for every good man." I stood up then and took my leave.

All the way to my car, I felt Sheila watching me from the window.

I don't know anyone named Helen.

Thirty-one

When the phone rang this time, I jumped to pick it up rather than wait for the machine.

"Miz Fortier?" At first I thought it was an obscene call because it was a whisper, a young black voice. "Got somethin' for you. Somethin' you want to know."

"What is this about?"

"I saw who dumped the dude down by Almonaster. Got the plate. Got the description."

"Why didn't you tell the police about this?"

"No way."

"They wouldn't give away your identity."

"But they would'n pay me no cash money. You gonna?"

(Everything is cash these days. Whatever happened to civic-mindedness?)

"Maybe. What did the man look like?"

"Hey, no way! You gotta meet me on the Mandeville Street Wharf wit' the cash money. *Then* I tell you sompin'."

"What's your name?"

"My name? I ain't tellin' you nuttin' 'bout no name."

"But I have to call you *something*."

"Yeah? Then, okay, you can call me . . . I'm *Bo*. Like 'Bo knows.' See?"

I mashed the disconnect button, then punched the number of Frank's office. A deep, resonant female voice answered and claimed he wasn't there.

"Margo Fortier," I said. "Tell Lieutenant Washington I'm on my way to meet a young black guy who's calling himself Bo at the Mandeville Street Wharf."

"We don't expect him to call in for an hour." She raised her tone slightly. "Are you sure you should go?"

"It's broad daylight on a busy wharf. What can happen?"

I hadn't counted on the wharf's being deserted today. I had naturally assumed some freighter would be docked there, some seamen walking around. (Damn the recession! Shipping's got so slow I'd be lucky to see a rowboat all day.)

I stood alone in the parking lot for several minutes before the huge front door of the warehouse rolled up to reveal a young man standing inside.

"Miz Fortier? Psst."

"Hello? Are you Bo?"

"Yeah." He laughed, inhaling in snorts. " 'Bo knows.' C'mon inside."

I stepped inside the warehouse, in which were stacked cardboard crates, ten high and labeled Air Popcorn Poppers.

Bo couldn't have been more than fourteen. His hair was pruned like a hedge into a pillbox shape, and as I drew closer I saw that his eyes were bright and drugged. I was put in mind of anencephalic monsters, children born without brains. Here was a child without humanity instead. A chemically made monster.

Instinctually, I kept several feet of distance between us.

"So what information do you have?"

"I got it raht heah!" Then suddenly Bo sprang at me like a tiger in the jungle. I turned and ran, screaming like a banshee, but he overtook me in seconds and gripped my arm tightly with both hands.

"Shut up, cunt!"

Still screaming, I tried to pull away, but in the next instant another boy emerged from the shadows behind him as though out of the air. My gut curdled as I realized this was the same pair who had stalked me on my walk home two nights before. Today, though, there was no convenient dog to bound to my rescue.

I shut up then and put all my energy into mentally cursing myself. Here I'd made the stupidest fucking mistake of my whole life and was about get my ass *killed*. So what was I supposed to do now? Fight? Go limp? Say a perfect Act of Contrition? Screaming was out of the question. There wasn't a soul around to hear, and besides, I hadn't the breath for it.

The decision not to do anything at all was made for me when the second boy reached inside his jacket and drew a pistol from his waistband.

"This is the reporter." The hedge head moved behind me as smoothly as his patron saint and twisted my arm. "Out for a big story."

"Reporter?" I was forced up on my toes. "Hey, not *me*. I just do this *gossip* column. Trash!"

"How we 'posed to do her?" the gunman asked. "Same like the dude in the dump?"

"Nah." Bo sneered. "Gimme the piece here." He took his friend's pistol and cocked it. "This time we 'posed to put her in her car and it be a accident."

(Yipe! How would a *liberal* handle this?)

I said, "Hey, we can talk this over. You're doing this for someone else, right? If it's a question of money, I can pay you more."

"Shut you face, bitch! We gettin' sompin' *better* 'n' money!"

"What's better than money?"

He was about to reply with a Buddy Rich imitation on my head when he was diverted by a shout from outside the warehouse.

"Hold it and don't *move!*"

"Shit!" The hedge head whirled toward the barked command with his gun cocked and fired a wild shot through the wide door. The next sound was the return shot from outside, not wild, and it hit Bo squarely in the chest. He was still on his way to the cement floor when his companion reeled and scrambled for the rear exit, right across the dock and into the river with a hard splash.

Then I was able to see my rescuers, though only in silhouette: two tall men holding automatic pistols and a short one between them who didn't need a weapon. That one I recognized.

"Rocco!"

Flanked by his bodyguards, Robert Fortunado walked through the smoke with his hands in his pockets.

"You oughta get a nose job, Cherry. That thing is bound to get you killed."

I enjoyed three deep breaths before going on with, "I didn't know this was your enterprise."

"It isn't. All the better reason to have the place watched real close."

He gestured for his henchmen to leave us alone, and they both marched outside. "My man told me he saw you sashay in here, so I thought I'd better drop over."

"I don't know how to thank you—or am I just being stupid?"

"Incredibly stupid." He moved over to one of the Popcorn Popper boxes, used his pocketknife to saw it open, and liberated a glassine bag.

"They're shipping it in from Hawaii." He snapped his fingers against the frosty white substance. "Ice."

"Is that something new?"

"The advanced stage of methamphetamine: the drug of the nineties."

"A new one? Cripe, I'd thought all the drugs had been invented already."

"Nuh-uh." Rocco shook his head. "They tell me this stuff

gives the longest-term high of any of them. For fifty bucks you can feel like Superman all day and all night."

"Priced for the mass market."

"Fun for the whole family. Even kids can afford ice. And it's easy to do. You don't have to inject it, no needles, no sterilizing."

"Just put it in your pipe and smoke it?"

"Yeah. The snag is distribution. The crap is being manufactured in Korea and brought in through Hawaii. They can't use Koreans for mules in New Orleans. Too easy to spot. They need some what you call 'indigenous personnel' to do the street sales. There's so much money in this crap, they don't even count it. They *weigh* it. And it's all tax-free. So they're recruiting from the projects. Twelve-year-old kids run fast, work cheap, and the police can't do anything to 'em." He inclined his head. "Bet this punk has a mother somewhere in the projects who's gonna be cryin' her eyes out on 'Eyewitness News.'" He put his hand on my shoulder to turn me to the door. "Let's get out of here, Cherry. We don't feel like explaining to your cop friend why we offed a teenage kid."

"You go ahead. I have to stay and wait for Frank."

"What the hell for?"

"This deal was personal, Rocco. It's the second time that same team tried to put out my light."

"If it wasn't about drugs, then what else? You must have been chasing one of your stories too hard."

"The only story I'm working on is the Eric Dowd case."

"So lay off it."

"But why would a black ice dealer have a stake in the murder of a white hippie that happened years before he was even born?"

Rocco prodded the corpse with his toe.

"Ask him."

Forty-five minutes later, Rocco was long gone, and Lieutenant Frank Washington stood on the same spot.

"Ice." He weighed one of the bags in his hand. "I didn't dream there was this much of the garbage in the whole region."

"The advanced stage of methamphetamine," I said, to display my new intelligence. "The drug of the nineties."

"This load would be worth millions." Frank turned away from the covered stretcher being carried off by two sturdy paramedics. "Certainly worth the lives of a few thousand black kids."

"Simply awful."

I wouldn't join him in the mourning box but couldn't say why.

"So, Margo, you had no idea who the dead boy was?"

"I thought his name was Bo."

"Hmmpf!" He turned away. "You don't know diddly."

Officer Prout wandered over and handed Frank a thin billfold sewn of red alligator.

"This belonged to the deceased." He snorted. "Not likely he bought it, though."

Frank grunted. "Is there a name in there?"

"School ID in the name of Henry Denson. The photo matches."

Frank folded his arms and looked stern. "So, Mrs. Fortier? You never talked to Henry Denson before?"

"Never until this morning. He called to say he had seen who dumped Ray Lowery up on Almonaster. He picked the meeting place."

"And when you got here?"

"He was already dead." Mentally I was crossing my fingers. I hated lying to Frank. Again. But then it wouldn't have been exactly prudent to discuss Rocco's participation.

He nodded slowly. "Fine. Now, let's adjourn to my unit for a private conversation, shall we?"

"Sure." I sort of skipped all the way to the police car, and, thoughtfully, he opened the right front door for me. I was feeling very important to be in on this vital investigation.

But my high spirits deflated when Frank settled into the driver's seat and pushed a button that closed and locked all the doors and windows. I'm a bit claustrophobic.

"Now, Mrs. Fortier, would you like to tell me again . . . ?" He turned toward me, and his voice was supersugary, like a parody of Good Cop. " . . . That you never spoke to Henry Denson before he called you . . . ?"

"Uh . . . right."

"And he was already dead when you got here?"

"Yeah."

"Then please tell me . . . " Now he narrowed his eyes and showed all his teeth. "How on earth you could know *that* voice on the phone belonged to *that* dead boy!"

At this point, Margie Albright would have gargled.

Thirty-two

The revolving lounge at the top of the Trade Mart has comfortable armchairs and a stunning view of the Greater New Orleans twin-span bridge, all lit up. I think it's the most inspiring place in the city and so the best site for a new romance. Or a renewed one.

I was holding Rocco's chubby hand and squeezed it for punctuation as I recounted my ordeal.

" . . . So I had to sit there and claim that I just *assumed* that the black kid I found was the same black kid I'd come to meet, dead or not."

My escort nodded and gazed past me, out the window.

"Did Washington believe you?"

"Not bloody likely. But at least he couldn't prove I was lying."

"You can't get past Washington; he's one of the smartest on the force, black or white."

"Yeah, Frank was always one of those terminally high achievers. He didn't need any affirmative action."

"Nobody does." Rocco gestured with his brandy. "They didn't start any affirmative action for white basketball players and rap singers."

"On the other hand . . . " I was listening to the piped-in music, the latest from Whitney Houston. (Gorgeous second generation of Cissy and Thelma.) "I don't even want to imagine American music without the black influence."

"Right, we'd probably be a nation of yodeling accordion players."

"Can you hear the words? 'All the man that I need.' "

"I swear." He held his palms up, the base of the thumbs well padded. "I don't remember even meeting the woman, and there she is going around singing about me."

I slipped my hand into his. "I like that one. 'All the man that I'll ever need.' "

We glanced over at a young couple outlined against the star-specked panorama, the male rumbling in his lowest register, the female giggling in her highest. Both looked young enough to be our children.

Rocco sighed heavily. "Doesn't love look stupid when it's two other people?"

I said, "We'll never feel that good again."

"Don't give up. Maybe we'll feel *better* because we can be clearheaded about it."

"Kids today take more time than we did. They have to do the blood test, the police check, the D&B . . . "

He rubbed my back and nodded. "Twenty years ago it was just 'Hi, I'm Rocco. Let's fuck.' "

"Back then we were all under thirty and immortal. I had my little prescription for the pill and figured I'd beaten biology."

"Biology is changed."

"In those days an unprotected intercourse could stick you with a baby. Now all it can do is kill you."

"We're a decaying world, Cherry."

I gazed out at the city, lighted high-rise buildings framed against the black sky. New Orleans is its most beautiful at night from high up here, far from the squalor and ugliness of the side streets, the project courtyards . . .

I can't cure them, so I'd rather not see them.

"You know, Rocco, I think my heart has atrophied." I squeezed his hand again. "The only thing that makes me cry anymore is that commercial about that nice boy with Down's syndrome who works at McDonald's."

"Well, sure. Me, too."

Looking at the world from way up here put mankind in cold perspective. What did it matter that one hippie was murdered twenty years ago when the whole human race is terminal?

THIRTY-THREE

Rocco pulled up in front of my house and turned off the engine. "I'll walk you to the door."

That wasn't a come-on. In the Ninth Ward, you always make sure a friend is locked safely inside before driving away.

I picked up my purse. "Julian flew to New York for a business conference. Would you like to come in for coffee?"

"Coffee?" Rocco took the key out of the ignition. "Yeah, sure. Right now I'm dyin' for coffee."

"And I'm dying to make you some."

Back in the kitchen, I ignored Julian's part of it, the stove and pots and so forth, and went right straight to *my* part, the coffeemaker. I measured three tablespoons of Community All-Purpose grind into the paper filter and poured water in the top.

As the water dripped through to change itself into coffee, I put place mats on the table and kept the conversation light with current events.

"How *about* that war. Do you believe those Iraqi pilots flying to Iran are all *defecting?*"

"Not a chance." Rocco turned his chair around and straddled it. "Hussein is just stashing his best planes across the border in neutral territory so they won't get blown to hell by SLAMs."

"David Letterman said next year's Baghdad Air Show will be held in Iran."

"Don't worry. Those planes will be back in Baghdad anytime Hussein wants."

"But Iran says they won't let them go."

"Believe it then. We can sure trust *them*."

"We're so civilized about this one." I opened the silver drawer and got Rocco a teaspoon with an engraved *F*. "I mean, who could imagine that our news people would be staying right there in Baghdad and reporting the war from the other side."

Rocco scowled. "Only what the other side *wants* reported. Every story is showing that disclaimer, 'Cleared by Iraqi censors.' "

"So we know it's one-sided. But don't you think it's fantastic that Peter Arnett interviewed Hussein in his bunker!"

"What for? He didn't learn anything."

"So just the fact that he *met* him made history! I mean, could you have imagined Chet Huntley interviewing Ho Chi Minh? Or Ed Murrow interviewing Hitler in *his* bunker?"

"Or Ben Franklin asking George the Third what kind of a tree he would be? No, not really. But that crap-head Hussein likes to watch himself on TV."

"He couldn't have been too concerned with his public image three weeks ago when he started pumping Kuwaiti oil into the Persian Gulf."

"That was something." Rocco loosened his tie. "Hussein spilled almost as much oil on purpose as Exxon does accidentally."

"CNN kept showing footage of this poor bird all covered with oil." I dug the cup and saucer out of the china cabinet. "I had an urge to get some Mr. Clean and scrub the poor thing down. I guess I felt more sorry for the bird than for the *human* war victims."

"Yeah?" Rocco tilted his chin up. "I wonder where they *really* shot that footage of the bird. They might have got it right around here."

"You're a habitual cynic."

"Nah, just spent my life keepin' my eyes open."

"Well, one good thing is coming out of this mess. Finally we have a black man who's viable for national office." I set our "heirloom" trivet on the table. "I'm tired of being told I'm a bigot because I wouldn't vote for Jesse Jackson."

He shook his head. "Won't make any difference. Colin Powell will be in the White House and we'll still have twenty million black crooks claiming they went bad just because they couldn't get an even break in this country."

"Excuse me." I put the coffee in front of him with the sugar bowl and pitcher of cream. "Would you like some pussy with that?"

"Yeah, I'll take a little. Thanks."

Mine is the master bedroom. It's twice the size of Julian's and more sensually appointed with a king-size poster bed, lots of pillows, and indirect lighting for the most romantic atmosphere.

When I was young I could just shuck my jeans behind any clump of bushes or in the back of a van and get it as good as it could be got. But now in the flower of my middle age the spirit has flagged and the stage setting has become important.

And the postgame conversation much more diverting.

"The people clamored for vice, so we used to sell it to them," Rocco was saying. "Gambling clubs, bookmaking, girls. . . . The customers had a good time; we made money. It seemed like it was all harmless except that it was illegal."

"And untaxable."

"We paid plenty taxes, believe me." He sat up against the bolster and folded his arms behind his head. "Almost everyone on the public payroll was on our payroll, too."

"That seems to have changed in twenty years."

"You don't mean corruption?"

"No, big shot. I mean *centralized* corruption. Nowadays every corner crack dealer has to pay off his own dirty cops."

"Even crooks have it worse in the nineties, Cherry. Is there *anything* that's better?"

"*You're* better. You last longer than when we were young."

"It *takes* longer."

Rocco hooked his right arm around me and pulled me against him so that we were touching from head to toe. I kissed his neck and twisted my fingers through the hair on his chest. "I love this. Hair on a man's chest is much sexier than on his head."

"You really think that?"

"Absolutely. Women, children, and eunuchs all keep their hair. Only real men go bald."

"Know what I like about you?" Rocco held me away from him so he could study my face in the light of pink diffusion. "You look wanton. Like you really *need* it, you know?"

"You mean like *desperate?*"

"Yeah. That really turns me on."

"Yeesh!"

THIRTY-FOUR

February 25, 1991

Frank passed me a mug shot that, for all I knew, could have been a generic all-purpose mug shot. They might even use the selfsame mug shot for every freaking suspect in the whole whacked-up country. I just looked blank.

"Maybe. Maybe not."

"Henry Denson lived in the Ninth Ward, only five blocks from your house. You sure you don't recognize him?"

"Frank, if Henry Denson were to come back to life tomorrow and surface in my bathtub, I *still* wouldn't recognize him."

"Try this one." Beside that photo, he placed another, indistinguishable from it. "This is Grover Jones, Denson's partner in crime."

"Couldn't prove it by me."

"Fortunately, we don't have to prove it by you. We picked up Jones, and he copped to being at the scene."

"Oh?" (Gargle time again. But I squared my shoulders and managed to look self-righteous.) "What kind of lies did *he* tell you?"

"Some interesting ones," Frank deadpanned. "One lie was that his friend was still alive when you arrived on the Mandeville Street Wharf."

"Really?" I fairly squawked. He didn't react to my reaction.

"Another lie was that you and Denson were having a friendly discussion when three white men burst in and shot him dead for absolutely no reason whatsoever."

"Wow." I scratched my head. "What an imagination."

"Yes. And here's a third lie that may amuse you even more. Jones said his friend Henry used to brag about being connected with the Mafia."

"Uh . . . yeah? I may laugh my head off at that one. *You* know bragging about Mafia connections is the surest sign you don't have any."

"That would be my first thought. But, if not Mafia, then who were those three?" Frank counted on his fingers. "Not black, not Asian, not Hispanic, but *white* men who blew young Denson away?"

"Geez, I don't know."

"Neither does Grover Jones. He claims the sun was behind the gunmen when they appeared, he only saw them for a split second, and besides, all white men look alike to him."

"So he'd—ah—never be able to identify them."

"I'm afraid not."

"Goodness, that's too bad."

"The Denson family has earned a lot of personal attention from this office." Frank picked up a stack of fan-feed paper, held the first page up over his head, and let the rest of it unfold in portions till the loose end reached his feet and began refolding into another stack on the linoleum. "They lived in a rental building off North Rampart. The mother and nine children."

"Where were the nine fathers?"

"No one knows. But it appears that Hattie Denson didn't need any man's help in raising her young. She was a second-generation welfare mother herself. So she raised all her daughters to follow her onto the public dole and all her sons to be criminals."

"On purpose?"

"Certainly. A ten-year old drug runner takes home a thousand a week and turns most of it over to his loving mom. They're living the American dream."

"Why didn't they tie Hattie Denson's tubes the first time she asked for a welfare check?"

"It's nice to dream about those measures, isn't it?" Frank smiled with one side of his mouth. "But they'll never be implemented."

"Okay, back to reality. How did a child of fourteen get access to a whole warehouse full of drugs?"

Frank let the first page of the record drop, and it landed neatly, folding itself on top of the stack.

"Denson's oldest brother, Harold, was known to us as the most active crack wholesaler in the city. After he died in prison last year, Henry took over his territory."

I picked up the pile of fan feed and placed it on his desk without looking. "The real mystery is what Henry Denson had to do with the man we knew as Eric Dowd."

"Don't go wandering down that road, Margo. Whoever put the hippie in the wall is at least forty years old now, and you can bet he's white."

Officer Prout wandered in then, fanning himself with a sheet of computer paper with green vertical stripes.

"Good news. Forensics checked Denson's Lincoln convertible for hair and fiber. We have all we need to prove Lowery's body was carried in the trunk."

I put on my hate-to-sound-stupid look.

"How could a kid that age have a car?"

Prout gave me his yes-you-*are*-stupid look. "The punk was too young to *drive* a car but not too young to buy one. Say, Chief, Hattie Denson is down at the desk screaming and carrying on like a gut-shot hyena."

"Sure she's screaming. Henry is the second son she's lost in a year."

"It ain't that. Hell, she can always make more kids. But she wants the Lincoln convertible back."

Frank smirked. "Tell her it's evidence. We keep it."

"Good deal. I'll really enjoy telling her that."

I watched Prout hustle out the door with a grin on his face and said, "That woman hasn't made many friends around here."

"As a crime matriarch, Hattie Denson makes Ma Barker look like June Cleaver." Frank put a giant clip on her file. "She's the one who popularized the famous 'brother switch' here in New Orleans."

"What's the 'brother switch'?"

"I'll give you an example. Her twelve-year-old son, Cory, broke into a neighbor's house, and the neighbor just happened to recognize him, so we were about to get the punk indicted. Then on trial day, Hattie Denson went sashaying into court with Cory's older brother, her thirteen-year-old son, Herman."

"And they looked exactly alike, right?"

"Exactly. So, before we could alert her, the witness fingered Herman as the burglar." Frank held his pen like a dagger and stabbed the air. Herman had the best of alibis; he was locked up at the time of the crime. So the victim's identification was thrown out. Case dismissed."

THIRTY-FIVE

Julian dropped his suitcase in the hallway and hurried to join me in the living room, sprinting the last few steps.

"What's the latest on the war?!"

"Why are you so anxious? Didn't they have the war in New York?"

"Not on the plane. We were out of touch."

Julian punched the set onto CNN.

"Over three hundred thousand Iraqui troops have surrendered so far," Bernard Shaw reported. "And Saddam Hussein appeared on Baghdad radio ordering his forces to withdraw from Kuwait."

Julian nodded. "That sounds encouraging."

But the subsequent translation of Hussein's remarks sounded a lot like a victory speech.

I was minded of the Newspeak idiom of the Nam era. When troops failed to hold a piece of real estate, they never retreated, nor were they withdrawn. Instead they were "redeployed" to safer ground.

Julian sighed and turned off the set.

"So what about you? How went your campaign for the affections of Rocco Fortunado?"

"Just take a gander." I led Julian into our dining room and pointed to the fresh new centerpiece gracefully, with the back of my hand, like Vanna pointing to a grand prize.

"White roses!" he sorted through them. "There must be ... um ... eight-ten-twelve ... two dozen of the things here. It looks like you made a hit with your gangster."

"He's a respectable businessman," I said snootily, and drew one of the roses from the bunch. "I really turn him on, too. You know what? Robert said I have the *Superdome* of pussies."

"And you think that's a compliment?"

I held the rose up to my cheek. "And right in the middle of the bouquet was a bottle of Diva. The perfume, mind you, not the cologne."

"Margo, the Superdome is the largest indoor sports arena in the *world*."

"He knows it's my favorite fragrance. I always wear it for him."

"I mean, the place is just *immense*."

Chloe Washington is the only person I know who still goes to church, so I dialed her number.

"Hi, Chloe. Julian and I are getting our pictures taken being a wholesome traditional couple."

"What do you want to do? Adopt my kids?"

"I hope it doesn't come to that. We're showing up at Mass, and I need to borrow a hat."

"Margo, I'll lend you one if you *want*, but you don't have to wear a hat to Mass anymore."

"I don't?"

"And I've got more news for you. They say it in English now."

I disconnected, picked up my research papers, and joined my husband in the living room. "I've arranged for the hat."

Julian kept his eyes on the TV screen.

"Great. Our troubles are over. By the way, I fed the dog."

"You shouldn't do that."

"Why not? You feed her."

"Yeah, but begrudgingly. If she has a modicum of sensitivity, she'll get the hint that she's not wanted here and move on. What's on the TV? Oh, cripe!"

He was watching one of those depressing French movies on Bravo. This one was about a poor hunchback who was trying desperately to irrigate his farm, and Yves Montand was a mean, terrible person who wouldn't let him, and it had a miserable, tragic ending. A perfectly dreadful movie. I don't know what those French can be thinking of.

If they have Yves Montand, why the heck don't they get him to *sing* something and cheer everyone up?

I didn't mind interrupting *that* awful thing and dropped my materials on the coffee table in front of Julian.

"I hoped you could help me study."

He pressed the remote control mute button. "Study what?"

"These are photocopies from the *Times-Picyune* of June nineteenth, 1970."

"What do they say?"

"For one thing, they say I could have bought you a suit at Rubenstein Brothers for a hundred and thirty-five bucks." I held up the ad for him. "See? It had wide stripes, natural shoulders, and lapels out to here."

He nodded. "I just threw one like that away about eight years ago."

"Eight years ago was like yesterday, right? And it used to be such a long time."

"It seemed that way."

"The earth keeps turning faster and faster while we stay in the same place. Family sitcoms go on the air, run for years, and get canceled and I don't even notice them."

"Not till the apple-cheeked child actors have grown into sullen young adults and got themselves booked on some felony charge." He picked up a grocery ad for Shasta drinks at forty-nine cents a six-pack. "Margo dear, ever since that poor dead hippie was discovered, you've been trying to slip back into 1970."

"I'm getting to understand the boy by studying the world he left behind."

"We *all* left that world behind, Margo."

"We didn't *mean* to, though, did we, Neg? Didn't we think it would stay the same?"

"We thought it would get *better* once our love generation came into power. There would be no more racism and no more ignorance or poverty because everyone would share. *That's* what we thought." He turned up the volume again and gave the film his full attention. Or tried to.

"It was 1970, Julian. We were all young then. We had invented ideals, and the times they were a-changin'. We all grew up and got older except one Eric Dowd, forever frozen in youth. He never has to know the times went and changed back."

"Don't envy him."

Thirty-six

I climbed into the back of the car because Julian was driving, and Buddy, our best staff photographer, was all loaded down with equipment, so he got the suicide seat.

My better half started grumbling immediately as he turned down Burgundy Street.

"Margo, it's much too hot to wear this wool suit."

"Stop complaining." I had to duck to keep Chloe's plume from being smooshed against the car ceiling. "Navy blue is the best color for a wholesome family man like you to wear to Mass."

"Won't make any difference on black-and-white film," Buddy said neutrally.

Julian was already sweating through his collar. "All right, Margo, you're staging this farce." He took one hand off the wheel to fan himself with his lapel. "Which church are we supposed to be seen coming out of? St. Vincent's is on the next block."

"No good," Buddy mumbled. "Sidewalk's too narrow, and I couldn't get far back enough for a good shot. Something high up with steps would be good. I'd like to get a full-length shot from underneath."

"Oh, look at St. Paul's!" I pounded Julian's shoulder. "That's a *beautiful* church, and it's got a new paint job."

Julian didn't slow down. "Look again—it's Lutheran."

"Oh, nuts! They should warn people."

"Well, think of someplace else. I'm melting."

The photographer met my eyes in the rearview mirror. "You two supposed to be Catholic?"

"Of *course* we're Catholic. How about St. Louis Cathedral?"

Buddy moved his head negatively. "*No* one would believe that was your regular church. St. Louis is a tourist's monument with a resident congregation of about five. Let's try Our Lady of Guadelupe on North Rampart."

"Good idea," Julian said through gritted teeth. "They have the shrine of Saint Jude. And I think I'll need him."

Our Lady of Guadelupe was a full-service operation and furnished free parking for car and kids. As our little party trooped out of the garage and crossed the island, the double doors of the church were pushed open and propped ajar.

"Yayy! We're here just in time for the end of Mass."

"Good enough." Buddy unhung his camera bag, took his position right on the edge of the curb, and squatted. "Ready when you are."

"Let's go." I grabbed Julian and steered us through the crowd of faithful who were flocking the other way. When we reached the front door, I turned us around.

"All right, Neg, just take my arm like you're sort of helping me down the steps and don't look at the camera."

"Of course I won't look at the camera. You think I'm an idiot?"

"Say, Margo?"

It was after midnight, and Julian was tuned to Channel 27, MTV.

"Look here. This show is about the making of the 'Voices That Care' video."

"That sounds interesting."

"You think so?" He waved me over. "Well, can you just tell me who those people are?"

The camera panned the crowd of earnest singing patriots and my husband shook his head in absolute bewilderment. "I recognize Stevie Wonder, of course, but who the devil are those others? I *knew* most of the people on the 'We Are the World' thing. That one had Ray Charles and Harry Belafonte. But this . . ." He waved his hands.

"Well, there's Fonzie. See?"

"Yes, I recognize *him,* and I see Michelle Pfeiffer from *The Fabulous Baker Boys.* Hey!" He leaned forward and pointed with his chin. "There's that *liar* from 'Saturday Night Live.' What's *he* doing there?"

"Oh, him. He's everywhere. If Saddam Hussein does a video, he'll be in *it.*"

"I can place the actors, I guess, but the singers . . . well, I must not have been looking when they got famous."

"Well, that's Brooke Shields there. She's not an actress *or* a singer."

"But at least she's famous," he allowed. "Who is the gorgeous hunk with the hair?"

"Michael Bolton. We've already seen him on 'Letterman.' "

"But why is he sitting all alone on those steps?"

"I guess he's too important to sing with the others, like Michael Jackson was last time."

"*No one* is too important to sing with Stevie Wonder."

"Except Michael Bolton."

"Who the *deuce* is Michael Bolton!?"

"*That* guy—unless he's George Michael."

"I'm going to bed."

"Go ahead."

If you want to stay young, so they say, you're supposed to keep up with the latest singers, but I've decided not to make the effort anymore. I was still trying to tell Milli from Vanilli when they were both exposed as not being singers at all.

I punched the tuner up to VH1, the music channel for adults, and caught my favorite of the current videos, "King of the Hill" by Roger McGuinn from the Byrds. It stars drop-dead-handsome Charles Rocket as an out-of-control coke-snorting crooked banker who gets led away in handcuffs in the last shot. Thus ever to crooked bankers.

Rocket is a good actor, but he had the misfortune to head the worst "Saturday Night Live" cast ever assembled, the mercifully short-lived '80–'81 company. In the last minute of one broadcast, Rocket committed the sin of saying "Fuck" on live network television. The show went into hiatus the next day, and the poor wretch has been paying for that mad second of hubris ever since.

The next video in the rotation was "More Than Ever" by the blond, long-haired Nelson twins, hard-rock second generation of Ricky. They're gorgeous boys, but, speaking for myself, I'd rather hear "Garden Party."

I finally switched over to AMC. Fred Astaire never changes, God bless him.

Thirty-seven

February 26, 1991

"Honestly, Margo!"

Rev. Reggie McCann blinked like a neon bulb coming on. "I don't suspect *you*. Do you suspect *me?*"

"Not really, it's just that everyone who was anywhere near Madame Julie's on June twenty-first, 1970, has to be a suspect. See?"

"Ah-hmm."

He was getting ready for a speech in ten minutes, so I tried to speak faster.

"I just made this list." I showed him the yellow pad. "And I had to put your name on it, but it's way down there, see?"

He held the pad at arm's length. "I see. I'm right here between Rocco Fortunado and Toby Castle. Interesting company." He dropped the pad on the dresser and picked up an eyebrow pencil. "But why would *I* have wanted to kill Eric? He was a scrumptious boy."

"That's sort of the point, Reggie. See, Eric Dowd was accused of beating a fai—uh—homosexual nearly to death in Pennsylvania. The homosexual refused to press charges, so Eric got clean away with it."

"Mmm-hmm?" The good reverend leaned toward the mirror, redefining his left eyebrow.

"So . . . theoretically . . . I mean, I'm just playing devil's advocate here, you understand. . . ."

"Be my guest." Now he worked on the right, making a smooth stroke.

"You might have been attracted to Eric because he was so scrumptious and all and made a pass at him. Then *he* might have responded in a violent way. Then *you* might have met violence with more violence. You were a lot bigger than he."

Reggie turned away from the mirror and grinned at me.

"Still am."

"The theory is that the murderer had to be pretty strong, and there were only three men working at Madame Julie's that month."

"And you count me? Well, I'm flattered to pieces."

"Plus you lived right upstairs. After hours you had the whole building to yourself."

"But if *I* am the nasty murderer, then how did the late, unlamented Ray Lowery come into it?"

"As a blackmailer. Suppose Ray threatened to inform your Christian adherents that you were the most flagrant queen on Bourbon Street."

"You don't get it, Margo." He held his hands up. "I'm blackmail-proof. Since I'm selling myself as a reformed sinner, the worse sins I can claim to be reformed from, the better I'll sound."

"So you admit to your past?"

"Why not? If I had been perfect all my life, I wouldn't need a religion." He smiled from sideburn to sideburn. "One would have formed around me."

I sailed into the cafeteria like a correspondent just back from the trenches. "I've learned something, Frank." I took a cruller from the serving plate and broke it into ladylike halves. "We can cross the good Reverend McCann off the list."

Frank stirred his coffee. "Is he another 'too nice a guy'?"

"Maybe not." I slid into my side of the booth. "But all the

time I was telling him about how he was a suspect, Reggie just sat there calmly drawing on his eyebrows, as steady as you please."

"And murderers, of course, don't do eyebrows."

"Not *that* well they don't."

"If it will help, we've finally got a mug shot from Pittsburgh." Frank pushed it across the table. "This was taken in 1966 when the victim was seventeen. Ever see him before?"

I held the photo at arm's length. "How would I know?"

"You're right. Dowd's own mother wouldn't recognize him. Two black eyes, a swollen face, his hair matted with blood. . . . It's the only mug shot in existence, and with our luck, they took it right after he resisted arrest."

"And obviously the cops resisted his resistance."

"Even if we had a good picture, he'd look completely different after twenty-five years."

"Why should he? *I* don't."

"No, Margo, *you* don't. But most people grow up." Frank pulled a more familiar photo out of his pocket. "Anyhow, you may have been right about your friend's character. We've just learned that the hippie in the wall was not Eric Dowd. At least not this man with the record from Pittsburgh."

"You can't tell from the picture."

"No, *I* can't. But Myra Birnbaum can. She superimposed this photo over an equal-size picture of the victim's skull, and they don't match." He tapped the photo of the sculpture. "This"—and then the mug shot—"was not he."

"But I remember the kid introduced himself to all of us. Why would an honest peacenik want to use the name of a fugitive felon?"

"Considering that we haven't a clue as to who he was, no one will ever have the answer to that one."

"I think one person would."

"Who, pray tell?"

"The real Eric Dowd."

"You're right." Frank pressed his lips together. "The cop killer from Pittsburgh must still be alive."

"Channel Six, your twenty-four-hour news source," said the fresh-faced young anchor. Then the screen was filled with what looked like a yearbook photograph. It was a face I knew.

"Ronald Dickson, the twenty-year-old son of Senator Tom Dickson, was found dead late last night in his room at the Omega fraternity house." Then came a night exterior of the frat house and ambulance attendants wheeling out a still, white-sheeted figure as robe-clad neighbors gawked and whispered.

"The medical examiner stated that young Dickson must have died of a drug overdose sometime yesterday . . . "

The next shot was of a clean-cut young man labeled "Omega Resident."

"We all tried talking to Ron about the drugs," the frat boy said earnestly. "But then he'd just laugh and say there was nothing wrong with doing cocaine. His own father was even working to get it legalized."

There followed video footage of the esteemed senator barreling through the throng of reporters, with tears flowing freely down both cheeks and wetting his collar. He reeled away from the proffered microphones.

Today he had no politics.

Thirty-eight

"Hey, Margo." It was Buddy on the phone. "I got a good picture of you and Julian, and I can send it downstairs in time for the next edition."

"Great. The caption has to read, 'Mr. and Mrs. Julian Fortier coming out of their parish church after Mass.'"

"That's done. Got a problem, though. The priest is in the shot."

"Great, the priest *should* be in the shot."

"Yeah, but this priest is looking at you two blankly and sort of scratching his head like he's never seen either of you before in his whole life and can't even begin to imagine what the hell you're doing on his steps."

"Okay, crop the priest out."

"But if I do that, the photo won't fit the format. Tell you what, Margo. I'll try to put a picture of something else over the picture of the priest. Would that be okay?"

"Great idea. Go with that."

"Maybe I could superimpose the statue from the shrine of Saint Jude."

"Fine. Just have it done for the next edition. Chop-chop.

Time's a wastin.' " I made the Okay sign for Julian. Then a split second after I hung up the phone, it rang under my hand.

"Mrs. Fortier? This is Lloyd Scorpus from 'Focus on People.' "

"What are you focusing on *me* for?"

"This is about the item in *Southern Lavender*. Everyone is talking about it."

"Not me."

Julian looked curious, but I wouldn't give anything away from my end of the conversation.

The phone intruder was trying to sound like the Washington press corps. "Would you or your husband make a brief statement for us on camera?"

"We wouldn't dream of it." I turned my back to Julian so he'd get no clue from my face.

"Mrs. Fortier, does your refusal to comment mean the charge is true? That your marriage is a sham?"

"That's preposterous!"

"Some people are saying that you don't have children because you're husband and wife in name only."

"So at least we're not like *your* parents."

"What do you mean by that, Mrs. Fortier?"

"We're *married*."

I hung up, switched on the answering machine, and smiled for Julian. "You know those salesmen."

He nodded gravely. "It's about me, isn't it?"

"Yeah." I try to keep bad news to myself, but this time he had me dead to rights. "Those media vultures don't ever want to let go of it."

"I thought if we ignored it, it would go away."

"No, we have to *make* it go away. I'll issue a public statement."

"You *can't*. It's indecent!"

"We have friends at the various TV stations. I'll just round them up for a press conference."

The machine answered the next call, but I felt obliged to take over when I recognized Jim Turner's voice, full and hearty.

"Hello there, Margo. I have some big news for you."

"I'm all ears."

"This is too big for the phone. How about coming to see me at home?"

Then he recited an address across the lake in Covington, the yuppie capital of south Louisiana.

Julian wrote it down for me, as he's the one with the Mont Blanc. "Sounds like he has a break in the hippie case."

"He'd freakin'-well better, if I'm supposed to drive twenty-six miles across the Lake Pontchartrain Bridge to see him."

I started punching the Touch-Tone.

"Who are you calling now?"

"My partner in crime detection. I'd rather be driven all that way than drive."

"So would everyone else."

Frank showed such an ill-humor even before we hit the causeway that I was sorry I had let him in on my big break in the case. By the time we reached the thirteen-mile mark his conversation had deteriorated to "Hmffs."

I asked, "Would you rather I drive?"

"I've seen you drive."

That meant no.

Jim Turner lived in a beautifully wooded area of Covington. But everything that grew naturally on his street had been uprooted or plowed under by the developer so the nearly identical tract houses could be constructed with rapid efficiency.

"Hi! I'm *Bonnie.*"

The woman who answered the door looked like the standard-issue wife for the upwardly mobile. She wore slacks, a cotton shirt with the tails on the outside, and sandals, the uniform of the young mother. Her naturally blond hair was contained by a red bandanna and framed a symmetrical set of features, insipid in their perfection. She was photogenically slender, with thin shoulders and no hips. I'd bet her father had connections. Men like Jim Turner don't marry idly.

"Oh, Lieutenant Washington! I want you to know I'm very active with the Police Athletic League. I'm on the board."

Frank nodded graciously. "I'm happy to hear that, Mrs. Turner."

"And Mrs. Fortier!" she gushed. "I just loved your column about the identical twins who were queens of Rex and Comus."

That column had been a sprightly, gurgling treatise about two rich and beautiful twenty-year-olds with pedigrees that would have impressed Louis Quatorze. I had bubbled on about the twins' riding trophies, charitable work, and distinguished forebears. I was not cynical enough to propose that their selection as 1991 parade queens would probably be the greatest distinction of their aristocratic lives.

Julian, as a member of both clubs, had voted for them.

Traditionally, the kings of Rex and Comus are flabby old men with money and power who have spent decades politicking for the distinction. Their queens are lovely, unblemished debutantes whose families began politicking on their behalf before they were born.

"I'm so glad you liked it."

I pegged Bonnie Turner as a wanna-be debutante. If her husband caught enough ambulances to keep the social game rolling and if she played it long and hard enough, maybe one of her daughters would get to be a maid of Rex's court and, following the plan through diligently, one of her granddaughters could possibly be elected a queen.

"Do you still live in the city, Mrs. Fortier?"

"Still and always."

She indicated her flat, manicured lawn with a sweep of her hand. "Life is so much more pleasant up here in Covington.

The streets are clean and safe. The neighbors are wonderful." Bonnie tilted her head brightly. "I bet you'll get out of the city sometime."

"Oh, I know I will."

"Wonderful. Well, I'll just pop in and tell Jim you're here."

With that, she turned her flat behind and bustled off.

Frank tilted his head. "*You* leave the city?"

"I'll have to, after I'm dead."

"I see. Then you do believe in hell?"

"Absolutely. And directly as I arrive there, the devil himself will toss me in his Peugeot and drive me right out to a suburban development just like this one."

" 'Little boxes made of ticky-tacky.' "

"Exactly. Then old Nick will drag me into a house just like this one here and introduce me to my husband, Todd, a flabby corporate lawyer, and my three freckled children."

Frank held up three fingers. "Jennifer, Scott, and Kimberly."

"Those would be the names, yes. Then finally, the devil will hand me the keys to my station wagon, tell me I carpool on Thursdays, and drive away again laughing and leaving me there to scream and scream in vain."

"Lost soul that you'll be."

"Hellooo!" Bonnie Turner came skittering back. "Jim is so excited that you're here. Come this way, please."

The man of the house met us at the door of his paneled den.

"Welcome to my humble abode. Hah-hah."

He was dressed in yuppie Saturday, polyester slacks and a short-sleeved print shirt.

He stuck out his hand. "I'm glad that you came, too, Lieutenant."

"My pleasure."

They did their macho handgrip thing, then parted with a slight recoil as though in mutual repugnance.

Frank and I sat facing Turner's desk, which, like the law

office, resembled a Vietnam War museum. Prominently displayed was a framed black-and-white snapshot of Turner's platoon, identically helmeted men with names written in ink across their shirts to differentiate them. Our intrepid host kept his dog tags in an American Legion ashtray as though he had just now taken them off.

Turner shoved an eight-by-ten glossy across the desk. "How do you like this?"

It was the most flattering photo I'd ever seen.

"It's the most flattering photo I've ever seen." I passed it on to Frank. "Is that for one of your newspaper ads?"

"It's my new campaign poster." Turner showed his teeth. "You know Senator Dickson's dropped out of the governor's race."

Frank's brow grooved into gray furrows.

"His free-drugs promotion pretty much fell apart."

"I won't make the same mistake."

"You're going to run?"

"Now that he's out, sure. Why not? I already have the best media crew in the South. They've been bringing in clients and money. They'll do just as well bringing in votes."

All of a sudden I felt like I was out on a really bad date.

"Excuse me . . . Uh . . . Did you call me over here—*all* the way over here—just to announce that you're running for office?"

"What else?"

Frank shot me a look that could kill a snake, and I stuttered on like Marion Lorne.

"I . . . we . . . thought you had some new information about the hippie in the wall."

"Oh, in reference to that . . ." Turner stroked his chin implant. "I remembered something that happened back in the club. It may not be significant, but I thought you should know."

"That's great!" Now I nodded reassurance at Frank, who

just put down the flattering photo and stared straight ahead. "Just the smallest incident could be important."

"Then here it is . . ." Turner waved his hands slowly like Matlock in a courtroom scene. "One night, late in June, Ray Lowery had got Eric to clean up the back room for him. I seem to remember he offered him a ten-spot."

Eric had often done odd jobs like that. "So?"

"But then after he finished the job and the club was closing, Ray told Eric he'd drank three dollars' worth of Cokes, so he was only getting seven bucks for the work."

"That sounds exactly like Ray."

"That's what I thought, so I didn't pay attention. I just left the two of them to fight it out and walked back alone to the fleabag on Canal. I can't say this for sure . . ." He shrugged with his arms outstretched like a Fugawe Indian. "But it's at least possible that that was the last time I saw Eric."

Frank had picked up the dog tags and was making them clink.

"If Lowery was the killer, you could have saved Eric's life."

"If it happened that night, yes. I'll always regret not waiting for him."

"You being an expert at unarmed combat."

"And armed combat, too," Turner smirked.

"You had plenty of practice, I hear. Your record says one of your buddies was killed right in front of you."

"Quon Loa. VC sniper. Up in a tall tree." The lawyer made a trigger-pulling motion. "Bang. My best friend, Jack Brown, for the body bag."

"You remember what day you were discharged?"

"Hell no, but it must have been April or May."

I was eager to get off the soldier talk because I had none of my own. "That narrows it down, Frank. Frank?"

He was frowning so deeply, his face would hold a spring planting. Then he came back to me. "What?"

"Sometime in April."

"Yes." He persisted with Turner. "So suppose one night

after hours, you were sitting alone in Madame Julie's, helping yourself to the bar whiskey and thinking about Jack Brown, dead, then in walks this hippie, alive. Maybe he makes a peace sign. Maybe he calls you a baby burner. . . ."

"So maybe, in a drunken rage, I hit him over the head and stick him in the wall?"

"He was," Frank said to his chest. "The victim was hit over the head."

Turner pounded the desk. "Hey, Lieutenant, when I came back to the world, I had no more taste for war. A lot of Nam vets put on their uniforms and marched right along with the peaceniks. And if I hadn't been too busy working for a living, I might have lined up with them."

Frank and I had passed the twenty-third-mile marker of the Lake Pontchartrain Bridge before I tried to get some conversation out of him.

"You've got to admit it was worth the trip."

"Oh sure. Turner tentatively places Ray Lowery as the last man to see the hippie alive."

"That's a good lead, don't you think?"

"A stunning lead. Especially since Lowery himself is in no mood to contradict."

"That does look sort of fishy."

"And we've already cleared the Lowery murder by arrest. So if I wanted to file away this old case, I could simply theorize that it was Lowery who killed the hippie in the wall."

"How conveenient."

"But that still leaves me to wonder *why* Lowery was killed. Henry Denson didn't have to mug people. The kid had the biggest cache of drugs in the history of the city. So why would he even waste his time?"

"Maybe he was getting something better than drugs," I ventured. "And better than money." I couldn't admit the punk himself had told me this but felt obliged to suggest it.

"What's better than money?" Frank asked, then answered himself. "Power."

"Sure, that leads us to . . . " I skidded to a verbal halt.

"That leads us to Rocco Fortunado first." Frank pointed one finger on the steering wheel, then another. "And second, to your friend Geoffrey Grant."

"Why him?"

"Because as an elected official, he has something the Densons want and need more than anything else." He took his eyes from the causeway to meet mine. "Parole power."

Thirty-nine

I took a deep breath of clean air before entering Felix's office.

"I've got you another story for the political page."

Felix coughed, waved away his smoke, and rasped, "Wha-at?"

"Jim Turner is announcing for governor."

"Why not?" (cough) "He's been running all his life. Friend of the people, decorated hero . . . "

"And just so's we don't forget his war record, he keeps a disabled vet in his front office as a living testament to his brave deeds."

"So, one more animal for the circus. Edwin Edwards wants to come back and steal even more. David Duke threw his hood into the ring. Now Jim Turner. . . . Who are you going to vote for for governor?"

"In Louisiana it's usually a choice among Larry, Moe, and Curly. I may spend Election Day indoors with the shades drawn."

"Me, too. Hey, there's something else, Margo. I saw your picture in today's Vivant section. You and Julian were coming out of the church."

"My gosh! Did they print that?" I smote my brow. "Yeesh!

I can't even have a private moment with my husband without someone running up and taking a picture."

"It was a good photograph, but there's one little thing I was curious about."

"What's that?"

"It looked like the statue of Saint Jude was standing behind the two of you, scratching his head. Strangest thing."

"I didn't notice."

Forty

Julian carefully lifted up a blind and peeked through.

"Oh, Margo? There's a whole *plague* of media creatures out there on the front lawn. Are you ready for them?"

"You kidding? I'm ready for a furshlugginer *royal wedding*."

I had on the most feminine dress in my wardrobe, all flowers and flounces. I had done an ultraprofessional makeup job, finishing with a wet sponge, and had my painted hair fluffed to a fare-thee-well.

I paraded out on the front porch, solemnly like for first Holy Communion, and stepped over to the dozen microphones set up in a stand.

"Mrs. Fortier?" called a chinless newsman from "Ramrod Weekly," "You promised us a statement."

I arranged my face to show no expression. (Real people don't display emotion for cameras. Only actors do that.) Then I tapped the closest microphone once, as though by mistake, to assure that it was on, and gave my best angle to the camera from Channel 4 (the station with the highest ratings).

"Thank you for allowing me to answer those cruel charges about my marriage."

Twelve mitts went up, and I waved them down.

There was a catch in my voice.

"I can say only that Julian and I have been very happily married for fifteen years." I paused one, two beats. "We have desperately wanted children." *Like we wanted steel spikes driven through our skulls.* "But I have been unable to conceive." *Because the little m-f's can't swim through two layers of latex.* "I can't understand why these people would say these hurtful things about my husband and my marriage that are totally false."

"Mrs. Fortier?" Someone held up a pen for attention. "Is your husband going to sue for libel?"

But I just smiled bravely and shook my head.

"I . . . I can't say any more. Thank you."

Then in a great demonstration of modesty, I crossed my arms in front of my chest and backed into the house, only stumbling once.

Julian was waiting inside the dimness, still peeking through the closed blinds.

"Great little speech." He reached in front of me to double-lock the door. "Do you think they believed it?"

"It doesn't matter whether they believed it, just so long as the proper words were said." I flopped onto the couch and kicked off my shoes. "Now, anyone who wants to presume you're straight is free to do so. Appearances are all that's important, anyway."

"So long as I don't suck cocks in the street and scare the horses."

"Now you understand."

February 27, 1991

The moon is void of course all day, just sailing through the sky, without aspecting any planets. This is not a day to make plans; they won't stick.

I rolled out of bed and staggered into the living room,

where my better half had the TV on at a courteously low volume.

"Great news, Margo." He turned up the sound. "Listen to this!"

"To repeat," some TV voice intoned. "Americans all across the country proudly rejoice in the glory of victory!"

"Did he say 'victory'?"

"That's exactly what he said!" Julian clapped his hands together. "Victory! The ground war lasted only a hundred hours, and now it's all over."

He was tuned to CNN to watch Liberation Day in Kuwait City.

Our generation always wanted a Normandy and a V-E Day of our own. Of course, we missed them in Nam, and Grenada was nothing but a hat fight. But here we were now watching the Allies parade through the streets with their tanks and jeeps to so much cheering and ecstatic flag-waving that I almost thought the war had been worth it.

(In the spirit of that man in the joke who would repeatedly hit himself on the head with a hammer because it felt so good when he stopped.)

The end of the war is a glorious, heady experience for all of us who have lived it vicariously since the coalition troops landed in Saudi Arabia, August 22. It was like a TV miniseries starring Peter Strauss. There were the pyrotechnics of missiles in the night sky over Tel Aviv, brave prisoners of war talking like robots for the video cameras, one villain, thousands of heroes, and the requisite happy ending: the victory parade through the recaptured city.

"You see that! Hussein is finished." Julian shook his finger at the shot of jubilant Kuwaitis setting fire to a building-high mural of the vanquished Saddam. "So it looks like your astrologer friends were wrong when they said the Gulf crisis would keep dragging on."

"I'm sure they're thrilled to be wrong."

I sat on the arm of his chair to watch the celebratory reactions from observers all over the world. What I enjoyed most was the CNN footage of the U.S. medics hauling in and patching up wounded Iraqi soldiers, some near death, all receiving the same dedicated care as their coalition counterparts. One corporal, a young black woman, explained, "They breathe just like we do."

Julian said, "Bring a little love into the world and there will be that much less room for hate."

I squeezed his shoulder. "Maybe there *is* a predilection toward humanity among humans."

"Score another for civilization and Christian values!" He held up clasped hands in a victory sign. "Those Iraqi soldiers will go home singing praises of Americans and ready to turn on Hussein."

"Great. I can't wait till they drag him through the streets and string him up, Il Duce–style."

"I don't think they're *that* Christian yet, Margo." He patted my knee. "But from a public relations standpoint, this was a great war. It didn't last long enough to get monotonous, and hardly anyone got killed."

"And as a bonus, some local boys will get work putting out those Kuwaiti oil well fires."

"I'd bet they'll let them burn long enough to give our own oil industry a boost."

Forty-one

I hoped the Catahoula had finally given up her vigil, but she was still dug in there on the sidewalk. I put down my leftover rice, flavored with some leftover gravy. She said thank you by licking my arm before starting in on the food.

"Tell you what, girl." I scratched her ears, which needed scratching. "I've got to run now. But if you haven't found yourself a gig by the time I get back, we'll make a deal." She sat whipping her tail, waiting for the terms. "See, you're just too ugly to pass for any dog of mine, so you can stay here, but I'm going to pretend like I'm keeping you for a friend. Okay?"

She agreed to this subterfuge with a pant and a wag.

"I guess we old bitches have to stick up for each other."

I usually don't chew gum in public, but now I crammed a big wad of it into my mush as I started up the car.

The elevator man left me off at Turner's floor, which seemed deserted. Inside the law office, Jack Gilley wasn't sitting at his desk. His computer terminal and all the others were neatly covered.

"Hello?" I heard first my own echo bouncing around the glossy painted plaster, then Jim Turner's voice in reply.

"Come in." He opened the door to his private office. "I was glad when you called for another interview. I've got some more ideas for my platform."

"I didn't expect you to be alone here."

"Hey, it's Liberation Day! An old soldier like me is bound to give his people the day off. Right?"

I walked past him into the office but didn't sit down. Instead I wandered around his "museum" and picked up his Colt 45 automatic.

"It's a lot different from the last day of *your* war."

"I was back home by then," he said behind me.

I put the pistol down and pulled a Time-Life book off the shelf. It fell open to a description of the Tet offensive. "But you still surround yourself with it."

"What can I say?" He leaned back in his chair. "Can't get those days out of my mind."

"Most men would at least try. Why keep all these books around?"

He narrowed his eyes. "I'm proud of my service. That's why."

"I have another theory." I slipped the book back into its place. "I think you need all these for *study*. Because you were never *near* Vietnam. Never in the service at all."

Turner's chair creaked as he bolted to his feet and moved toward me. "You think I'm a phony veteran?"

"It's more than that. I think you're the *real* Eric Dowd."

"That right? And I think you're a pretty smart broad." In less than a second he lunged past me, and the Colt 45 was in his hand.

"That's a pretty good answer." I stayed icy calm. "Twenty years ago, you were wanted for murder up in Pittsburgh."

"A serious murder, too. Worse luck." He tilted the barrel up. "I thought the dude was just another hophead with too much bread, so I blew him away. I was going through his pockets for my money when I found the badge. Turned out he was a narc."

"The police get annoyed when you kill one of their own."

"So they say." Turner shook his head. "The Northeast was no place for me that season, so I popped the ignition in a Corvair and headed south. I wasn't really following any plan till I saw some soldiers in uniform, hitchhiking. That gave me the idea." He walked over to the door, closed and locked it. "So after that, whenever I spotted a serviceman about my size, I'd pick him up and interview him."

"You were shopping for a uniform."

"Most of the men were headed home, or back to a base. Those were no good for my purposes. I had to keep trying till I finally found one who wasn't expected anywhere."

"The real James Turner."

"He'd just got his discharge, and there were no family ties. Better than that, he'd been accepted at the University of New Orleans for the fall semester on the GI Bill. And nobody knew him down here. Corporal Jim Turner's future looked pretty good. Eric Dowd's looked pretty bad."

"So your plan was to rip off Turner's identity."

"But I had to learn his history first and then make the switch as unsuspicious as possible."

"How did you get him to cooperate?"

"I claimed I was a draft dodger on the lam and made him a proposition. If he'd just let me wear his uniform and use his name to get a job, I'd support us both till school started up in August. I would pay the bills, and he could just hang out. He bought the idea."

"So that's where he was getting his money. Then you bleached your hair to match his description."

"I matched his picture pretty close, too. No one looks very hard at those. Then we got adjacent rooms in that fleabag on Fourteen Hundred Block, and I learned all I had to know about being Jim Turner."

"All the time you were planning to kill him once you'd got the necessary details."

"There couldn't be two of us."

"But he upset your timetable when he told you he'd made one of the girls pregnant."

"Right. First I just told him to forget it. The broad was a tramp, and the kid probably wasn't his, anyway." He looked disgusted at the recollection. "But the asshole was set on marrying her."

"He knew he needed his own identity back to make it legal."

"I wasn't going to lose what I had; it was all set up too perfectly. So I couldn't let him walk out of there. The construction job was a lucky break."

"Eric Dowd's yellow sheet said you had worked in construction."

"I just pried off those cedar panels and propped him up inside with a couple of ten penny nails through his shirt." He rubbed a smudge off the barrel of the pistol. "Then I installed the panels back on top of him. Took me a good two hours to do a neat job."

"It funny no one noticed the closet came out a foot shorter."

"Yeah, I had a few bad months worrying about that. Or maybe that someone would figure out where the smell was coming from. But after a few years, I thought they'd never find him. What made you come after me?"

"I knew I was getting close when the late Henry Denson tried to kill me. Finally I realized that only *you* could have sent him."

"How do you figure?"

"You had access to his kind. 'Friend of the people' Jim Turner likes to sue the police department on behalf of felons."

He smiled wryly. "Brutalized citizens."

"Frank told me Henry's older brother died in prison last year. So I'll just bet you approached his family and asked if they wanted to sue the parish for wrongful death."

"They didn't." Without taking his eyes from mine, Turner

reached over and unplugged his phone. "Harold Denson was a known rapist, and another inmate carved a shiv out of a dinner fork and killed him in self-defense. But the mother saw how an important lawyer could be useful in a lot of ways."

"No doubt. So Henry was willing to cooperate. It would have looked like just one more crack murder."

"Common as roaches in New Orleans."

"But the likes of Henry Denson wouldn't have passed through the Silver Lamp unchallenged."

"No shit. The little monkey didn't even know his *way* to Metairie."

"So you killed Samantha yourself."

"I had to take the risk."

"But why her?"

"Because I read her message off your answering machine."

"What? How did you get in my house?"

"I didn't have to go *near* your house. I had your phone number, and you had an old model answering machine." With his free hand, he pulled a beeper out of his pocket and held it up.

"I forgot the machine came with one."

"I keep a whole drawerful of these suckers in assorted tones, so I just called your number. When I got the machine, I went through beepers till I hit one that played the messages. I heard that crazy woman say she checked some records and found out I was still alive." Turner dropped the beeper back in his pocket. "So I made an appointment for a private reading."

"She meant the *akashic* records, not real ones. She thought you were reincarnated as a baby."

"How's that?"

"Poor Samantha was just a New Age psychic dingbat, no threat to you at all."

"What can I say? My mistake." He grinned and waved the gun. "Now, I'd bet you came here to trap me with a tape recorder in your purse."

"Matter of fact I did."

"Makes no difference. I'll erase it after."

"After what?"

"You always were stupid," he smirked. "Cherry."

"Well, maybe I am. But *you* would be *really* stupid if you fired that gun."

"Oh, is that so?" The smirk didn't uncurl. "Why?"

"Because I jammed a whole package of Trident cinnamon chewing gum down the barrel."

"What?" Then he pointed the barrel right to his face and looked. "You fucking . . . "

"So maybe you could shoot me, but just as maybe, the stock would blow up in your face."

"So? Maybe I have nothing to lose by trying." He leveled the barrel at my face, and in the longest second of my life, I wondered if I had time for a perfect Act of Contrition or if just *wanting* to make one would count.

Then the window shattered.

"Hold it! Don't move a hair."

"Frank?"

There he was, Lieutenant Washington, the most uncomfortable man I ever saw, crouched on the fire escape with his police special in both hands and aimed right at the lawyer's startled face.

In the next second, the office door was battered off its hinges with one blow of a ramrod operated by two young patrolmen as the lawyer did a quick calculation, weighing the criminal justice system against instant bloody demise, and dropped his pistol.

Officer Prout followed his men in and took charge of the collar, furnishing handcuffs while a subordinate told the prisoner he had the right to remain silent.

"I'm not waiving *anything*," Turner bellowed. "I want my lawyer."

"You can call him the minute we get downtown. Margo?" Prout turned to me. "You want to help?"

"Sure. What can I do?"

"Go get the chief off the fire escape."

"Check." I sprinted over to the window and unlocked it.

"Lord, I'm too old for this," Frank was muttering, shielding his face from sharded glass. "Next time, a new guy gets the fire escape." I pushed up what was left of the window, and Frank managed to unfold himself and get over the sill. "Front door next time. Kick me if I don't."

"I didn't dream you were following me!"

"We weren't, Margo. We were following *Turner*." Carefully, he brushed glittering splinters off his right sleeve. "Now he's getting a ride to Tulane and Broad and you're getting a ride home."

"No, I can drive myself."

He pointed to my hands, which had just begun to shake so hard, I looked like Don Knotts on the old "Steve Allen Show."

"You sure you want to drive yourself?"

"Nooo?!"

Meekly I accompanied him downstairs and let him put me in his car. We were already past Esplanade when I finally asked, "What made you suspect Turner?"

"Remember when I asked him what day he got out of the service?"

"Uh, yeah. He said he couldn't recall."

"Right. Now, Margo, I did a tour in Nam myself. And there's not a man in my unit who wouldn't remember the *exact minute* he was released from the service. A GI is more likely to forget his own birthday."

"Oh."

"So, I memorized the number on his dog tags, sent it to Washington, and got back an ID." Frank reached across me into the glove compartment for a single piece of paper. "Jim Turner was an exemplary soldier, all right. He won every medal in that display case. But look here." The document Frank handed me was only a fax copy, but the photo of the earnest young soldier was unmistakably the original hippie. That same boy who had walked me to the bus stop twenty-one years before.

"Then he wasn't a draft dodger at all. He was a hero."

"Right."

"But if you were on to Turner, why didn't you tell me?"

"Why in heaven's name would I tell you?"

"He was a killer."

"All I knew was that he was a phony. And I couldn't even prove that because he could just claim to be a different Corporal Turner. Records get mixed up. And what's more we had a decorated veteran, Jack Gilley, swearing up and down that he knew the man in Lai Kie. That didn't add up."

"Sure it did. I mean, just suppose *you* were a crip—uh—physically challenged war vet in desperate need of a job and the very guy who might *give* you that job says, 'Hey, weren't we together in Lai Kie?' Wouldn't *you* remember serving with him?"

"I see your point." Frank raked his hair. "I guess I'd remember *sleeping* with him, if I *had* to."

"So when he got Gilley's job application saying he'd been in Nam during the same period as the real Turner, the phony bought himself a human credential."

"But I couldn't go into court with my opinion, could I? We needed something to roll on, and we got it today. Thank you."

"Don't mention it. But now I feel like a blue-striped fool."

"Don't feel bad, Margo. After all, it was *you* who solved the case. You identified the victim and led us to the killer. Without you, that poor skeleton would have been buried without a name." Then he glowered at me in the rearview mirror. "But your idea of confronting Turner by yourself with nothing but a recorder and chewing gum was just plain—"

"Inappropriate."

"Try stupid. Unforgivably stupid."

"But maybe stupid enough to get me out of gossip and into real news, once Felix gets a load of this tape."

"He's not going to get a load of it anytime soon. It's evidence."

"Oh, fuck!"

"Sorry. Give it here."

Well, he *had* saved my life, so with a genteel minimum of cursing, I rewound the tape and slapped it into his outstretched paw. "Hope you choke on it."

"Thank you." He slipped it in his pocket.

I leaned back on the headrest as we passed the railroad tracks. "You know what I'd really enjoy, Frank?"

"What's that?"

"I'd like to *personally* go back into that law office, scoop up all those old war medals, and bring them to Sheila Casey for her son."

"Someone will have that pleasure. Maybe it will be you. Here comes the end of the line."

Frank turned left on Piety and pulled up to the curb in front of my house. I opened the door without help, then swung my legs around smoothly, the way a lady does. My neighbor Ida was out walking her cat again and waved when she saw me.

"Well, Mrs. Fortier, you see that dog is gone!"

"Good. Maybe some rabbit hunter took her."

"Oh no. It was the dogcatcher in his white truck."

"The dogcatcher?"

"Well, sure." Ida blinked. "And you know that dog didn't even have the sense to run away from him? She just sat right here on the sidewalk and let him *catch* her with a loop on a stick."

I fell back into the squad car. "Frank! You've got to drive me to the dog pound!"

"The what?"

"Fast!" I was bouncing in my seat. "It's Wednesday!"

"Wednesday?!" But Frank was yanking the wheel as he asked it, then pulled away from the curb and headed toward St. Claude, pressing the speed limit. I was winding up so tight my head almost scraped the dome light.

He turned left two blocks before Poland to avoid the stoplight, made a right, then another left, and careened into the dog pound parking lot. Before he even came to a full stop, I pulled the door open with all my weight, burst through, and ran to the desk.

"A Catahoula! They brought it in?"

The Hispanic secretary was concerned enough to stand up and hurry to the counter.

"There was a Catahoula bitch. An old one, but . . . "

"That's it! She's mine!"

"They said she didn't belong to anyone. I'm sorry." The girl shook her head. "She must be gone now."

"Gone?!"

"Today's the day they euthanize the old dogs no one wants."

"But I *do* want her! Please! I *promised* her!"

The girl glanced at her watch. "Wait." And pressed her intercom button. "There may still be a chance." There was a buzz but no response, and my guts turned to water. "Chuck was late getting in, so . . . " Another buzz and still no response. She picked up her keys. "I'll try in the back."

Maybe, thank heaven, my panic was contagious. Half running, the secretary reached the door to the kennel and unlocked it; I followed her through without an invitation, toward the far right aisle that was death row for unadoptable strays.

"Chuck!" I heard her call to a bearded man in a plaid shirt who held on to three dogs by ropes: a white-muzzled shepherd, a mangy weimaraner, and the third, mine, still alive. "We want the Catahoula!"

I bent and slapped my knees. "Here, Brutus!"

The Catahoula leapt and turned in midair, and if Chuck

hadn't released his hold then, she would have dragged him on his belly all the way up the row as she shot out to meet me.

I was on my knees by the time she reached me, but she knocked me the rest of the way down with her front paws, jumping and panting, sloshing and wagging.

"Don't worry, girl, I won't be ashamed of you, because you're going to be *beautiful*. Every night I'll feed you meat and fat and you'll fill out and I'll brush you all over and your coat will shine."

The secretary spoke over our heads. "If you want that old dog, you can bail her out for thirty-five dollars."

Then I barely heard Frank's voice behind me.

"You may as well start the paperwork, miss. It looks like I'll have two passengers for the ride back."

My new dog was whipping her tail so furiously that her rear end swayed with centrifugal force as I scratched her head.

"Then I'll buy you the prettiest white collar with colored stones all around it. You'll be the most beautiful hound in town, you'll see." She licked my face.

"Beautiful . . ." I told her again.